# High-Powered, Hot-Blooded

# High-Powered, Hot-Blooded



Susan Mallery

KENNEBEC
CHIVERS

This Large Print edition is published by Kennebec Large Print, Waterville, Maine, USA and by AudioGO Ltd, Bath, England.
Kennebec Large Print, a part of Gale, Cengage Learning.

The text of this Large Print edition is unabridged.
Other aspects of the book may vary from the original edition.
Set in 16 pt. Plantin.

LIBRARY OF CONGRESS CATALOGING-IN-PUBLICATION DATA

Mallery, Susan.
High-powered, hot-blooded / by Susan Mallery. — Large print ed.
p. cm. — (Kennebec Large Print superior collection)
ISBN-13: 978-1-4104-2657-4 (pbk.)
ISBN-10: 1-4104-2657-2 (lpbk.)
1. Businessmen—Fiction. 2. Large type books. I. Title.
PS3613.A453H54 2010
813'.6—dc22
2010006979

BRITISH LIBRARY CATALOGUING-IN-PUBLICATION DATA AVAILABLE
Published in 2010 in the U.S. by arrangement with Harlequin Books, S.A.
Published in 2010 in the U.K. by arrangement with Harlequin Enterprises II B.V.

U.K. Hardcover: 978 1 408 49156 0 (Chivers Large Print)
U.K. Softcover: 978 1 408 49157 7 (Camden Large Print)

Printed and bound in Great Britain by
CPI Antony Rowe, Chippenham, Wiltshire.

1 2 3 4 5 6 7 14 13 12 11 10

Dear Reader,
There are so many things I love about this time of year. The crisp days and nights, the holiday decorations, the tempting special foods. Mostly I love curling up in front of a fire with a mug of hot chocolate and a delicious romance novel. As the craziness descends, I try to schedule a few at-home evenings to indulge myself.

For my hero Duncan Patrick, the holidays aren't the least bit special. He doesn't believe in tradition or family or even being nice to anyone. He doesn't see the point. For him, life is all about the bottom line. He's been so successful, he's completely lost what really matters.

I'll admit I love heroes like that. Guys who are totally clueless and don't see what's headed right for them. It's not the love of a good woman that changes their lives — it's *loving* a good woman. It's going to take someone special to get Duncan's attention and Annie McCoy is exactly who he needs.

Now, Annie isn't looking for a powerful, determined, stubborn guy to warm her nights, but that's exactly who she's going to get. I think she'll thank me later.

I hope you love reading this story as much as I enjoyed writing it. However you celebrate at this time of year, may your days be joyous and happy and may you spend them with those you love.

*Susan Mallery*

# Prologue

*CEO knocks out the competition.*

*CEO Duncan Patrick has once again knocked out the competition. The shipping billionaire ends the year with two more acquisitions, including a small European trucking company and a very profitable railroad line in South America. With Patrick Industries dominating the world transportation market, one would think the wealthy billionaire could afford to be gracious, but apparently that's not the case. For the second year in a row, Duncan has been named meanest CEO in the country. Not surprisingly, the reclusive billionaire declined to be interviewed for this article.*

"This is unconscionable," Lawrence Patrick said, slamming the business newspaper onto the boardroom table.

Duncan leaned back in his chair and stifled a yawn. "Did you want me to do the interview?"

"That's not the point and you know it."

"What is the point?" Duncan asked, turning his attention from his uncle to the other men on the board. "Is there too much money coming in? Are the investors unhappy with all the proceeds?"

"The point is the press loves to hate you," Lawrence snapped. "You bought a mobile home park, then evicted the residents, most of whom were elderly and poor."

"The mobile home park was right next to one of the largest shipping facilities we own. I needed the land for expansion. The board approved the purchase."

"We didn't approve seeing old ladies on television, crying because they had nowhere to go."

Duncan rolled his eyes. "Oh, please. Part of the deal was providing the residents with a new mobile home park. Their lots are bigger and the area is residential, rather than industrial. They have bus service right outside the main gate. We paid all the costs. No one lost anything. It was the media trying to create a story."

One of the other board members glared at him. "Are you denying you bankrupt your competition?"

"Not at all. If I want to buy a company

but the person who owns it won't sell to me, I find another way." He straightened. "A legal way, gentlemen. You've all invested in my company and you've seen extraordinary profits. I don't give a damn what the press thinks about me or my company."

"Therein lies the problem," his uncle told him. "We *do.* Patrick Industries has a terrible reputation, as do you."

"Both are undeserved."

"Regardless. This isn't your company, Duncan. You brought us in when you needed money to buy out your partner. Part of the deal is you answer to us."

Duncan didn't like the sound of that. He was the one who had taken Patrick Industries from a struggling small business to a world-class empire. Not them — him.

"If you're threatening me," he began.

"Not threatening," another board member said. "Duncan, we understand that there's a difference between ruthless and mean. But the public doesn't. We're asking you to play nice for the next few months."

"Get off this list," his uncle said, waving the paper at him. "It's practically Christmas. Give money to orphans, find a cause. Rescue a puppy. Date a nice girl, for once. Hell, we don't even care if you really change. Perception is everything. You know that."

Duncan shook his head. "So you don't care if I'm the biggest bastard in the world, as long as no one knows about it?"

"Exactly."

"Easy enough," he said, rising to his feet. He could play nice for a few months, while raising enough money to buy out his board. Then he wouldn't have to care what anyone thought of him. Which was how he preferred things.

# One

Annie McCoy could accept the flat tire. The car was old and the tires should have been replaced last spring. She could also understand that little Cody had eaten dirt on the playground, then thrown up on her favorite skirt. She wouldn't complain about the notice she'd gotten from the electric company pointing out, ever so politely, that she was overdue — again — and that they would be raising her rates. It was that all of it had happened on the same day. Couldn't the universe give her a sixteenth of a break?

She stood in front of her sagging front porch and flipped through the rest of the mail. No other bills, unless that official-looking letter from UCLA was actually a tuition bill. The good news was that her cousin Julie was in her first year at the prestigious college. The bad news was paying for it. Even living at home, the costs were enormous and Annie was doing her best to help.

"A problem for another time," she told herself as she walked to the front door and opened it.

Once inside, she put her purse on the small table by the door and dropped the mail into the macaroni-and-gold-spray-paint-covered in-box her kindergarten class had made for her last year. Then she went into the kitchen to check out the dry-erase bulletin board hanging from the wall.

It was Wednesday. Julie had a night class. Jenny, Julie's twin, was working her usual evening job at a restaurant in Westwood. Kami, the exchange student from Guam, had gone to the mall with friends. Annie had the house to herself . . . at least for the next couple of hours. Talk about heaven.

She walked to the refrigerator and got out the box of white wine. After pouring a glass, she kicked off her shoes and walked barefoot to the backyard.

The grass was cool under her feet. All around the fence, lush plants grew and flowered. It was L.A. Growing anything was pretty easy, as long as you didn't mind paying the water bill. Annie did mind, but she loved the plants more. They reminded her of her mom, who had always been an avid gardener.

She'd barely settled on the old, creaky wooden swing by the bougainvillea when she heard the doorbell ring. She thought about ignoring whoever was there, but couldn't bring herself to do it. She went back inside, opened the door and stared at the man standing on her porch.

He was tall and powerfully built. The well-tailored suit didn't disguise the muscles in his arms and chest. He looked like he could have picked up money on the side working as a bouncer. He had dark hair and the coldest gray eyes she'd ever seen. And he looked seriously annoyed.

"Who are you?" he demanded by way of greeting. "The girlfriend? Is Tim here?"

Annie started to hold up her hands in a shape of a T. Talk about needing a time-out. Fortunately she remembered she was holding a wineglass and managed to keep from spilling.

"Hi," she said, wishing she'd thought to actually take a sip before answering the door. "I'm sure that's how you meant to start."

"What?"

"By saying 'hello.' "

The man's expression darkened. "I don't have time for small talk. Is Tim McCoy here?"

The tone wasn't friendly and the words didn't make her feel any better. She set her glass on the tiny table by the door and braced herself for the worst.

"Tim is my brother. Who are you?"

"His boss."

"Oh."

That couldn't be good, she thought, stepping back to invite the man in. Tim hadn't said much about his relatively new job and Annie had been afraid to ask. Tim was . . . flaky. No, that wasn't right. He could be really sweet and caring but he had a streak of the devil in him.

The man entered and looked around the living room. It was small and a little shabby, but homey, she thought. At least that's what she told herself. There were a few paper turkeys on the wall, and a pair of pilgrim candlesticks on the coffee table. They would come down this weekend when she got serious about her Christmas decorating.

"I'm Annie McCoy," she said, holding out her hand. "Tim's sister."

"Duncan Patrick."

They shook hands. Annie tried not to wince as his large fingers engulfed hers. Fortunately the man didn't squeeze. From the looks of things, he could have crushed her bones to dust.

"Or ground them for bread," she murmured.

"What?"

"Oh, sorry. Nothing. Fairy-tale flashback. The witch in Hansel and Gretel. Doesn't she want to grind their bones to make her bread? No, that's the giants. I can't remember. Now I'll have to look that up."

Duncan frowned at her and stepped back.

She couldn't help chuckling. "Don't worry. It's not contagious. I think weird things from time to time. You won't catch it by being in the room." She stopped babbling and cleared her throat. "As to my brother, he doesn't live here."

Duncan frowned. "But this is his house."

Was it just her or was Duncan not the brightest bulb? "He doesn't live here," she repeated, speaking more slowly. Maybe it was all the muscles. Too much blood in the biceps and not enough in the brain.

"I got that, Ms. McCoy. Does he own the house? He told me he did."

Annie didn't like the sound of that. She crossed to the club chair by the door and grabbed hold of the back. "No. This is *my* house." She felt more than a little panicked and slightly sick to her stomach. "Why are you asking?"

"Do you know where your brother is?"

"Not at the moment."

This was bad, she thought frantically. She could tell it was really bad. Duncan Patrick didn't look like the kind of man who dropped by on a whim. Which meant Tim had done something especially stupid this time.

"Just tell me," she said quickly. "What did he do?"

"He embezzled from my company."

The room tilted slightly. Annie's stomach lurched and she wondered if she was going to join little Cody in throwing up on her skirt.

Tim had stolen from his employer. She wanted to ask how that was possible, but she already knew the answer. Tim had a problem. He loved to gamble. Loved it way too much. Living only a five-hour drive from Las Vegas made the problem even more complicated.

"How much?" she asked in a whisper.

"Two hundred and fifty thousand dollars."

Her breath caught. It might as well be a million. Or ten. That was too much money. An impossible amount to pay back. He was ruined forever.

"I can see by the look on your face, you didn't know about his activities."

She shook her head. "The last I heard, he

loved his job."

"A little too much," Duncan said drily. "Is this the first time he's embezzled?"

She hesitated. "He's, um, had some problems before."

"With gambling?"

"You know?"

"He mentioned it when I spoke with him earlier today. He also told me that he owned a house and that the value exceeded the amount he'd stolen."

Her eyes widened. "No way. He didn't."

"I'm afraid he did, Ms. McCoy. Is this the house he meant?"

Now she really was going to be sick. Tim had offered the house? *Her* house? It was all she had.

When their mother had died, she'd left them the house and an insurance policy to split. Annie had used her half of the insurance money to buy Tim out of the house. He was supposed to use the money to pay off his college loans and put money down on a place of his own. Instead he'd gone to Vegas. That had been nearly five years ago.

"This is my house," she said firmly. "Mine is the only name on the deed."

Nothing about Duncan's cold expression changed. "Does your brother own other property?"

She shook her head.

"Thank you for your time." He turned to leave.

"Wait." She threw herself in front of the door. Tim might be a total screw-up but he was her brother. "What happens now?"

"Your brother goes to jail."

"He needs help, not prison. Doesn't your company have a medical plan? Can't you get him into a program of some kind?"

"I could have, before he took the money. If he can't pay me back, I'll turn him over to the police. Two hundred and fifty thousand dollars is a lot of money, Ms. McCoy."

"Annie," she said absently. It was more money than he knew. "Can't Tim pay you back over time?"

"No." He glanced around at her living room again. "But if you'd be willing to mortgage your house, I would consider dropping the charges."

Mortgage her . . . "Give up where I live? This is all I have in the world. I can't risk it."

"Not even for your brother?"

Talk about playing dirty.

"You wouldn't lose your house if you made regular payments to the bank," he said. "Or do you have a gambling problem, too?"

The contempt in his voice was really annoying, she thought as she glared at him. She took in the perfectly fitted suit, the shiny gold watch that probably cost more than she made in three months and had a feeling that if she looked out front, she would see a pretty, new, fancy, foreign car. With good tires.

It was too much. She was tired, hungry and this was the last problem she could deal with right now.

She grabbed the electric bill from the inbox and waved it in front of him.

"Do you know what this is?"

"No."

"It's a bill. One I'm late on. Do you know why?"

"Ms. McCoy . . ."

"Answer the question," she yelled. "Do you know why?"

He looked more amused than afraid, which really pissed her off. "No. Why?"

"Because I'm currently helping to support my two cousins. They're both in college and have partial scholarships, and their mom, my aunt, is a hairdresser and has her own issues to deal with. Have you seen what college-age girls eat? I don't know how they get it all down and stay skinny, but they do. Follow me."

She walked into the kitchen. Surprisingly Duncan came after her. She pointed at the dry-erase board. "You see that? Our family schedule. Kami is an exchange student. Well, not really. She was in high school. She's from Guam. Now she goes to college here. She's friends with my cousins and can't afford her own place. So she lives here, too. And while they all help as much as they can, it isn't much."

She drew in a breath. "I'm feeding three college-age girls, paying about half their tuition, for most of their books and keeping a roof over their heads. I also have an aging car, a house in constant need of repair and plenty of student loans from my own education. I do all of this on a kindergarten teacher's salary. So no. Taking out a loan on my house, the only asset I have in the world, is not an option."

She stared at the tall, muscled man in her kitchen and prayed she'd gotten through to him.

She hadn't.

"While this is all interesting," he said, "it doesn't get me my two hundred and fifty thousand dollars. If you know where your brother is, I suggest you tell him to turn himself in. It will go better for him that way than if he's found and arrested."

The weight of the world seemed to press down on her shoulders. "No. You can't. I'll make payments. A hundred dollars a month. Two hundred. I can do that, I swear." Maybe she could get a second job. "It's less than four weeks until Christmas. You can't throw Tim in jail now. He needs help. He needs to get this fixed. Sending him to prison won't change anything. It's not like you need the money."

The ice returned to his cool, gray eyes. "And that makes it all right to steal?"

She winced. "Of course not. It's just, please. I'll work with you. This is my family you're talking about."

"Then mortgage your house, Ms. McCoy."

There was a finality to his tone. A promise that he meant what he said about throwing Tim in jail.

How was she supposed to decide? The house or Tim's freedom. The problem was she didn't trust her brother to do any better if she mortgaged the house, but how could she let him be locked away?

"It's impossible," she said.

"Actually, it's very easy."

"For you," she snapped. "What are you? The meanest man on the planet? Give me a second here."

He stiffened slightly. If she hadn't been staring at him, she wouldn't have noticed the sudden tension in his shoulders or the narrowing of his eyes.

"What did you say?" he asked, his voice low and controlled.

"I said give me a minute. Maybe there's another choice. A compromise. I'm good at negotiating." What she really wanted to say was she was good at negotiating with unreasonable children, but doubted Duncan would appreciate the comparison.

"Are you married, Ms. McCoy?"

"What?" She glanced around warily. "No. But my neighbors all know me and if I yell, they'll come running."

The amusement returned. "I'm not here to threaten you."

"Lucky me. You're here to threaten my brother. Practically the same thing."

"You teach kindergarten you said. For how long?"

"This is my fifth year." She named the school. "Why?"

"You like children?"

"Well, duh."

"Any drug use? Alcohol problems? Other addictions?"

An unnatural love for chocolate, but that was really a girl thing. "No, but I don't . . ."

"Any of your ex-boyfriends in prison?"

Now it was her turn to be pissed. "Hey, that's my life you're talking about."

"You didn't answer the question."

She reminded herself she didn't have to. That it wasn't his business. Still she found herself saying, "No. Of course not."

He leaned against the chipped counter and studied her. "What if there *is* a third option? Another way to save your brother?"

"Which would be what?"

"It's four weeks until Christmas. I want to hire you for the holiday season. I'll pay you by forgiving half of Tim's debt, sending him to rehab and setting up a payment plan for the remainder of the money. To be paid by him when he gets out."

Which sounded too good to be true. "What do I have that's worth over a hundred thousand dollars?"

For the first time since entering her house, Duncan Patrick smiled. The quick movement transformed his face, making him seem boyish and handsome. It also made her very, very nervous.

She took a step back. "We're not talking sex, are we?" she asked desperately.

"No, Ms. McCoy. I don't want to have sex with you."

The blush came on hot and fast. "I know

that I'm not really the sex type."

Duncan raised an eyebrow.

"I'm more the best friend," she continued, feeling the hole getting deeper and deeper. "The girl you talk to, not the girl you sleep with. The one you take home to Mom when you want to convince her you're dating a nice girl."

"Exactly," he said.

What? "You want to introduce me to your mother?"

"No. I want to introduce you to everyone else. I want you to be my date for all the social events I have going on this holiday season. You'll show the world I'm not a complete bastard."

"I don't understand." He was hiring her to be his date? "You could go out with anyone you want."

"True, but the women I want to go out with don't solve my problem. You do."

"How?"

"You teach small children, look after your family. You're a nice girl. I need nice. In return your brother doesn't go to jail." He folded his arms across his chest. "Annie, if you say yes, your brother gets the help he needs. If you say no, he goes to jail."

As if she hadn't figured that out on her

own. "You don't play fair, do you?"
"I play to win. So which will it be?"

# Two

While Duncan waited for his answer, Annie grabbed a kitchen chair and pulled it over to the refrigerator. She reached the overhead cupboard and pulled out a box of high-fiber cereal. After opening it, she removed a plastic bag filled with orange and brown M&M's.

"What are you doing?" he asked, wondering if the stress had pushed her over the edge.

"Getting my secret stash. I live with three other women. If you think chocolate would last more than fifteen seconds in this house, you're deluding yourself." She scooped out a handful, then put the plastic bag back in the box and slid the box onto the shelf.

"Why are they that color?"

She looked at him as if he were an idiot, then climbed down from the chair. "They're from Halloween. I bought them November first, when they're half off. It's a great time to buy seasonal candy. They taste just as good. M&M's are my weakness." She popped two in her mouth and sighed. "Better."

Okay, this was strange, he thought. "You had a glass of wine before," he said. "Don't you want that?"

"Instead of chocolate? No."

She stood there in a shapeless blue sweater that matched her eyes and a patterned skirt that went to her knees. Her feet were bare and he could see she'd painted little daisies on her toes. Aside from that, Annie McCoy was strictly utilitarian. No makeup, no jewelry to speak of. Just a plain, inexpensive watch around her left wrist. Her hair was an appealing color. Shades of gold in a riot of curls that tumbled past her shoulders. She wasn't a woman who spent a lot of time on her appearance.

Which was fine by him. The outside could easily be fixed. He was far more concerned about her character. From what he'd seen in the past ten minutes, she was compassionate, caring and led with her heart. In other words, a sucker. Happy news for him. Right now he needed a bleeding-heart do-gooder to get his board off his back long enough for him to wrestle control from them.

"You haven't answered my question," he reminded her.

Annie sighed. "I know. Mostly because I still don't know what you want from me."

He pointed to the rickety chairs pushed up against the table. "Why don't we sit down."

It was her house — she should be doing the inviting. Still Annie found herself dragging her chair over to the table and plopping down. Politeness dictated that she offer him some of her precious store of M&M's, but she had a feeling she was going to need them later.

He took a seat across from her and rested his large arms on the table. "I run a company," he began. "Patrick Industries."

"Tell me it's a family business," she said, without thinking. "You inherited it, right? You're not such a total egomaniac that you named it after yourself."

The corner of his mouth twitched. "I see the chocolate gives you courage."

"A little."

"I inherited the company while I was in college. I took it from nothing to a billion-dollar empire in fifteen years."

Lucky him, she thought, thinking she had nothing to bond with. Scoring in the top two percent of the country on her SATs was hardly impressive when compared with billions.

"To get that far, that fast, I was ruthless," he continued. "I bought companies, merged them into mine and streamlined them to make them very profitable."

She counted out the last M&M's. Eight round bits of heaven. "Is that a polite way of saying you fired people?"

He nodded. "The business world loves a success story, but only to a point. They consider me too ruthless. I'm getting some bad press. I need to counteract that."

"Why do you care what people say about you?"

"I don't, but my board of directors does. I need to fool people into thinking I have a heart. I need to appear . . ." He hesitated. "Nice."

Now it was her turn to smile. "Not your best quality?"

"No."

He had unusual eyes, she thought absently. The gray was a little scary, but not unattractive. If only they weren't so cold.

"You are exactly what you seem," he said. "A pretty, young teacher with more compassion than sense. People like that. The press will like that."

She'd been with him, right up until that

last bit. "Press? As in press?"

"Not television media or gossip reporters. I'm talking about business reporters. Between now and Christmas I have about a dozen social events I need to attend. I want you to go with me. As far as the world is concerned, we're dating and you're crazy about me. They'll think you're nice and by association, change their opinion of me."

Which all sounded easy enough, she thought. "Wouldn't it just be easier to actually act nice? This reminds me of high school when a few people worked really hard to cheat. They could have spent the same amount of time studying and gotten a better grade without any risk. But they would rather cheat."

His dark eyebrows drew together. "My reasons are not up for debate."

She picked up another M&M. "I'm just saying."

"If you agree, then I'll arrange for your brother to enter rehab immediately, under the conditions we discussed. He'll get the second chance you seem to think he deserves. However, if you let on to anyone that our relationship isn't real, if you say anything bad about me, then Tim goes directly to jail."

"Without collecting two hundred dollars."

"Exactly."

A deal with the devil, she thought, wondering how a nice girl like her got into a situation like this. Of course, her being a nice girl was apparently the point. She sighed.

The sense of being trapped was very real. As was the knowledge that while she was expected to take care of her cousins, Tim and apparently even Duncan Patrick, no one ever bothered to take care of her. Or worry about her.

"I'm not lying to my family," she said. "My cousins and Kami have to know."

Duncan seemed to consider that. "Just them. And if they tell anyone —"

She nodded. "I know. Off with their heads. Have you been through any seminars on teamwork or communications? If you worked on your people skills, you might . . ."

The gray eyes turned to ice. She pressed her lips together and stopped talking.

"You agree?" he asked.

Did she have a choice? Tim needed help. She'd tried to talk him into getting it before, but he always blew her off. Maybe being forced to spend some time in a safe place would make a difference. As the alternative was him being charged with a felony, she didn't see that she had a choice.

"I will," she began, "act as your adoring

girlfriend between now and Christmas. I will tell anyone who will listen that you are kind and sweet and have the heart of a marshmallow." She frowned at him. "I don't know anything about you. How am I supposed to fake being in a relationship?"

"I'll get you material."

"Won't that be happy reading."

He ignored her comment. "In return, Tim will get the help he needs, fifty percent of the debt will be forgiven and he'll have a reasonable payment plan for the rest. Do you have an appropriate wardrobe?"

She nibbled on the last M&M. "Define appropriate."

He looked at her with a thoroughness that left her breathless. Before she could react, he'd scanned her battered kitchen, his gaze lingering on the warped vinyl flooring.

"Someone will be in touch to arrange a session with a stylist," he said. "When the month is over, you can keep the clothes." He rose.

She stood and trailed after him. "What kind of clothes?"

"Cocktail dresses and evening gowns." He paused by the front door and faced her.

"I have the dress from my prom."

"I'm sure you wouldn't be comfortable wearing it at one of these events."

"Is this really happening?" she asked. "Are we having this conversation?"

"It is and we are. The first party is on Saturday night. My assistant will call you with the information. Please be ready on time."

He dwarfed her small living room, looking too masculine for the floral-print sofa and lacy curtains. She would never have imagined a man like him in her life, even temporarily.

"I'm sorry my brother stole from you," she said.

"He's not your responsibility."

"Of course he is. He's family."

For a second Duncan looked like he was going to say something, but instead he left. Annie closed the door behind him and wondered how she was going to tell her cousins and Kami what she'd gotten herself into now.

Saturday morning both Jenny and Julie stared at Annie with identical expressions of shock, their green eyes wide, their mouths hanging partially open. Kami looked just as surprised.

"What?" Julie asked. "You did what?"

Annie had put off telling them as long as she could. She'd hidden the binder that had been delivered on Thursday, sliding it under her bed, then pretending it didn't really exist. Her first "date" with Duncan was that night, so she was going to have to read it sooner rather than later.

"I agreed to go out with Tim's boss for a month. We're not really dating each other," she added hastily. "We're pretending until Christmas. I'm supposed to help his image."

But she still wasn't clear on how *that* was supposed to happen. Did Duncan expect her to give interviews? She wouldn't be very good at it. She could easily stand up in front of a room of five-year-olds, but a crowd of adults would make her nervous.

"I don't understand," Kami said, blinking at her. "Why?"

Jenny and Julie exchanged a look. "This is all about Tim, isn't it?" Jenny asked. "He's in trouble."

"Some," Annie admitted. "He, ah, embezzled some money. But Duncan is going to get him into rehab and that will help."

"Him, not you." Julie tucked her light brown hair behind her ears. "Let me guess. Tim somehow threw you under the bus on this one. What did he tell his boss about you?"

"It wasn't me, specifically. It was . . ." She cleared her throat. While she didn't want to tell her cousins what had happened, she believed in speaking the truth. Well, except when it came to her secret M&M stash.

She quickly explained about the two hundred and fifty thousand dollars, how Duncan would forgive half the debt and allow Tim to make payments on the other half when he got out of rehab and was working again.

Julie sprang to her feet. "I swear, Annie, you're impossible."

"Me? What did I do?"

"Gave in. Let Tim do this to you again. You're always getting him out of trouble. When he was seven and stole from the mini market by the house, you took the fall and paid them back for the candy bars. When he was in high school and cutting class, you convinced the principal not to suspend him. He needs to face the consequences of what he's done."

"He doesn't need to go to jail. How will that help?"

"If the pain's big enough, then maybe he'll learn his lesson."

Jenny nodded, while Kami only looked uncomfortable.

"He needs help," Annie said stubbornly. "And he's my brother."

"All the more reason to want him to grow

up and be responsible," Julie said.

Annie sighed. "I promised."

When her mother had been dying, she'd made Annie swear she would look after Tim, no matter what.

The twins exchanged another look.

"There's no getting around that," Kami told them. "You know how Annie gets. She always sees the best in people."

Annie stood and touched Julie's arm. "It's not that bad. I'm dating a really rich guy for a month, going to fancy parties. Nothing more."

All three girls looked at her. Annie felt herself starting to blush.

"Nothing," she repeated. "No sex, so don't even go there." She smiled. "I wouldn't have told you except I'll be gone a lot and eventually you'd notice. In the meantime, I kind of need your help. Duncan is sending a stylist to take me shopping for cocktail dresses and a couple of formal gowns. I won't need them after this month, but I get to keep them. So I thought you three might want to come along and give me your opinions. What with you being able to borrow them when I'm done."

As she expected, there was a general shrieking as all three of them jumped up and down, yelling.

"Seriously?" Jenny asked.

"Uh-huh. The stylist is due here any second and we're going shopping. So you want to come with me?"

They'd barely had time to agree when the doorbell rang. Jenny and Julie ran to open the door.

"Dear God," a man said. "Tell me Duncan isn't dating twins. Although you two are gorgeous. Have you thought about going into modeling?"

The twins giggled in response.

Annie went out into the living room where a tall, thin blond man stood looking over her cousins.

"Love the hair," he said, fluffing Julie's ends. "Maybe a few more layers to open up your face and give your hair volume. Try a smoky eye. You'll be delish." He looked past them to Annie and raised his eyebrows. "Now you look exactly like a stereotypical kindergarten teacher, so you must be Annie. What were you thinking, agreeing to help someone like Duncan? The man is a total ruthless bastard. Sexy, of course, not that he would ever notice me." He smiled. "I'm Cameron, by the way. And yes, I know it's a girl's name. I tell my mother it's the reason I'm gay."

He glanced over her shoulder as Kami

came in the room and he sighed. "I don't know who you are, honey, but you're giving these beauties a run for their money. Yummy."

Kami laughed. "Get real."

"I am real. The realest."

Annie introduced the girls. Cameron sat on the worn sofa in the living room and pulled out a couple of folders.

"Come on, little teacher," he said, patting the cushion next to him. "We have to go over the schedule. Duncan has fifteen social events between now and Christmas. You'll be with him at all of them."

He passed her one of the slim folders. "You got the background information, didn't you?"

She nodded, although she'd only read the basic bio. "Impressive. He put himself through college on a boxing scholarship."

Cameron's hazel eyes widened slightly. "You sound surprised."

"I was. It's not traditional."

"His uncle is Lawrence Patrick. The boxer."

"I've heard of him," Julie said. "He's, like, old, but he was really famous."

Annie had heard of him, as well. "Interesting family," she said.

"Duncan was raised by his uncle. It's a

fascinating story, one I'll let him tell you himself. You're going to be spending a lot of time together."

Not something Annie wanted to think about as she took the second folder Cameron offered. This one contained a questionnaire she was to fill out so Duncan could pretend to know all about her.

What had she been thinking, agreeing to this craziness? But before she could even consider backing out of the deal — not that she would — Cameron had ushered them all to the stretch limo waiting to take them shopping.

Five hours later, Annie was exhausted. She'd tried on dozens and dozens of dresses, blouses, pants and jackets. She'd stepped in and out of shoes, shrugged at small, shiny evening bags and endured a bra fitting from a very stern-looking older woman.

Now she sat with foil in her hair, watching pink polish dry on her nails. When they'd moved from shopping to a day spa, she'd been relieved to know she could finally sit down.

Cameron appeared with a glass of lemon water and a fruit-and-cheese plate.

"Tired?" he asked sympathetically.

"Beyond tired. I've never shopped so much in my life."

"People underestimate the energy required to power shop." Cameron settled in the empty salon chair next to her. "Getting it right takes effort."

"Apparently." While she'd thought all the outfits had fit okay, he'd insisted the store seamstress tuck and pin until they were perfect.

Cameron handed her a sheet of paper. On it was a list of the outfits, followed by the shoes and bags that went with each. She laughed.

"You must think I'm totally inept, although I'll admit I'm not sure I could remember this myself."

"I couldn't stand for you to clash. Putting a look together requires a lot of skills. It's why the good stylists make the big bucks."

"So you're famous?" she asked.

He smiled modestly. "In my world. I have a few celebrity clients I keep happy. Several corporate types like Duncan, who want me to keep their wardrobes current without being trendy. Not that Duncan actually cares what he wears. He's such a typical guy."

"How did you meet?"

Cameron raised his eyebrows. "We were college roommates."

If Annie had been drinking her lemon water, she would have choked. "Seriously?"

"I know. Hard to imagine. At least we never wanted to hook up with the same person. I was an art history major back then. I lasted a year before I realized fashion was my one true love. I moved to New York and tried to make it as a designer." He sighed. "I don't have the patience for creating. All that sewing. So not my thing. I took a job as a buyer at an upscale department store. Then I started working with the store's really exclusive customers. The rest, as they say, is history."

Annie tried to imagine Duncan and Cameron sharing a college dorm room, but she couldn't get her mind around the idea.

"What about you?" he asked. "How did you get involved with the big bad?"

"Is that what you call him?"

"Not to his face. He might hit me." But Cameron was smiling as he spoke and there was affection in his tone. "So what happened?"

She told him about Tim and the money. "I couldn't let my brother go to jail," she said. "Not when there was a chance to save him."

"Honey, you are too nice by far. Be careful Duncan doesn't chew you up and spit you out."

"You don't have to worry. This is business. I'm not interested in him personally."

"Uh-huh. You say that now, but Duncan is very charismatic. A friendly word of advice. Don't be fooled by the polite exterior. Duncan's a fighter. You're not. If there's a battle, he's going to win."

"You're sweet to worry, but don't. Even if I did fall for him —" something she couldn't begin to imagine "— he wouldn't respond. Seriously. I can't imagine that I'm his type."

"You're no Valentina."

"Who?"

"Valentina. His ex-wife. Stunning, in a scary girl-snake kind of way. Cold. Remember that line from *Pretty Woman*? About being able to freeze ice on someone's ass? That's Valentina."

She was surprised to hear that Duncan had been married, although she probably shouldn't be. He was successful and in his thirties. It made sense that he'd found someone.

"How long have they been divorced?"

"A couple of years. She scared me." He shivered. "So enough about Duncan. What about you? Why isn't a nice girl like you happily married?"

She reached for a strawberry. A question for the ages, she thought glumly. "I've had two serious relationships. Both times the guy left, each claiming he saw me more as a friend than as the love of his life."

She spoke lightly, as if the words didn't matter, as if she wasn't still hurt. Not that she missed either one of them. Not anymore. But she was beginning to wonder if there was something wrong with her. Something missing. The two relationships had lasted a total of four and a half years. *She'd* been in love, or so she'd thought. She'd been able to imagine a future, marriage, children. Those men were the only two she'd slept with and for her, the sex had been fine. Maybe not as magical as she'd heard it described by friends or in books, but still very nice.

But it hadn't been enough. Not the sex or her heart or any of it. Both of them had left. And that they'd said practically the same thing had her wondering.

"I don't want to be the best friend," she whispered fiercely.

Cameron patted her hand. "Tell me about it."

Annie was grateful beyond words that Hector, the genius at the salon, had styled her hair for the evening. He'd blown out her usually curly hair into a sleek cascade of waves that fell past her shoulders. Hector's assistant had done her makeup as well, so all she had to do was pull on the dress and step into the right shoes. Cameron had suggested a cocktail dress for the event. Now Annie stared at it and wondered if she had the nerve.

The dress was simple enough — sleeveless with a sweetheart neckline. Fitted, although not tight, and falling midthigh. It was the latter that made her want to squirm as she stared at herself in the mirror above her dresser. If she kept the mirror straight, she looked fine. Of course she could only see herself from the waist up. If she tilted the mirror down, she could see to her ankles and there was way too much leg showing.

Telling herself that by many standards, the dress wasn't even that short didn't help. She was used to skirts that fell closer to her ankles than her thighs. Of course, that was in the classroom where she was constantly bending over small desks or sitting on the floor. This was different.

Unfortunately the girls weren't around to ask. They'd gone out to the movies, leaving her to decide on her own. She could always change her clothes, but she didn't know what else would be appropriate for the party.

Before she could decide what to do, the doorbell rang. She glanced at the clock radio on her nightstand. Duncan was about ten minutes early. She would be wearing the dress she had on.

She stepped into her high heels, teetered for a second, then walked into the living room. Not sure what Duncan was going to have to say or what to expect from the evening, she drew in a deep breath and pulled open the door.

But the man standing there wasn't her date and he didn't look happy.

"What the hell did you do?" Tim demanded as he pushed past her into the house. "Dammit, Annie, you don't have the right to force me to go to one of those places."

"I see you finally decided to talk to me," she said coolly. "I've been leaving messages for three days." Ever since she and Duncan had made their deal.

Her brother faced her, his blue eyes flashing with anger. "You had no right."

"To do what?" she asked, feeling her own temper rise. "Help? You got into this, Tim. You stole money from your boss. How could you?"

He shifted slightly and dropped his gaze to the floor. "You wouldn't understand."

"I'm sure that's true. You have a problem. It's either rehab or jail."

"Thanks to you," he said bitterly.

She put her hands on her hips. "This is not my fault. I'm not the one who gambled and I'm not the one who told Duncan Patrick this house was yours. You stole and lied, Tim. You were willing to risk everything on a roll of the dice."

"I play cards."

"Whatever."

He glared at her. "You're my sister, Annie. You're supposed to help me, not throw me into some institution. What would Mom say?"

A low blow, she thought, more resigned than angry. "She would think you're a big disappointment. She would tell you that it was time to grow up and take responsibility."

Tim didn't even flinch. "It doesn't have to be like this," he said. "You could mortgage the house. It's half mine, anyway."

"It *was* half yours. I bought you out, remember? I'm tired of this, Tim. Tired of you expecting me to bail you out. I've always taken care of you and you've never been grateful or tried to change."

"You owe me." Tim moved closer. He was a lot bigger and taller. "You're going to mortgage the house, Annie. One way or the other. Do you hear me?"

She was too surprised to be afraid. Before she could figure out what to do next, Duncan walked through the half-open door.

"McCoy," he said.

Tim spun to face his boss. "What are you doing here?"

"I have an appointment with your sister."

Tim swung back to Annie, then looked her up and down. "You're going out with him?"

She nodded.

Tim's mouth twisted into a bitter smile. "Figures. I'm getting screwed and you're going on a date. Nice. Talk about ignoring your family."

The accusation burned down to her belly. "You don't know what you're talking about," she whispered. "This is about saving our family, something you don't care about."

Duncan grabbed Tim's arm. "She's right. As we discussed, you'll report to the treatment facility by nine tomorrow morning or there will be a warrant for your arrest."

Tim looked between them. "You're in this together. You're selling me out with this bastard? Dammit, Annie."

Duncan stepped between them. "Enough, McCoy. It's time for you to leave. Remember, by nine in the morning."

"Why wait?" Tim asked bitterly. "I'll go now."

"That's probably for the best."

Tim shook off Duncan's hand, then walked to the door. He paused and glanced back at her. "Do you even care?"

Annie pressed her lips together and refused to answer. Tim would manipulate her if she gave him the chance. She'd never been able to stand up to him, but maybe it was time to start learning how.

She squared her shoulders. "Good luck, Tim. I hope this works."

He glared at her. "It doesn't matter if it does, Annie. Either way, I'm never going to forgive you."

# Three

Duncan drove toward the hotel. Annie was silent, but he was aware of her next to him. He could inhale the scent of her subtle and feminine perfume. When he turned his head to the right, he caught a glimpse of her sleek thighs. Every now and then he heard a soft sigh.

"Are you mad at me or Tim?" he asked.

"What? Neither of you." She shifted toward him. "Mr. Patrick, I really appreciate your help with Tim. And he will, too. Eventually."

Unlikely, Duncan thought. But he'd been wrong before. Maybe rehab was what Tim needed. If it didn't work, he would screw up again and find himself in jail.

"I've been calling him all week," she admitted. "Trying to explain. Today is the first time I've seen him since we made our deal. He was so angry."

"You know he's lashing out at you because

it's safe, right?" he asked. "He can't admit he has a problem, so it has to be everyone else's fault."

"I know, but it was still hard to hear."

Tim was damn lucky to have Annie for his sister, Duncan thought. Unlikely he would recognize that, either.

"You going to be all right?" he asked.

"You mean can I still do my job?" she asked with a smile. "Yes. As well as I could have before Tim showed up." She bit her lower lip. "I'm not very good at this sort of thing."

Hell of a time to admit that, he thought, amused by her honesty. "Going to parties? There's not much of an expectation. Look pretty and smile adoringly at me. You got through college. This should be easy by comparison."

"There's a little more to it than that," she said. "Or aren't I expected to hold a conversation?"

"You're talking just fine."

"You're less scary than a room full of people I don't know."

"Then maybe you should call me Duncan instead of Mr. Patrick."

Her breath caught. He liked the sound. It was unexpected and sexy as hell. The kind of sound a woman made when . . .

He stopped himself in midthought. Hold on there, he told himself. Annie McCoy was many things, but sexy? He slid his gaze across her bare thighs. Okay, yeah, maybe sexy applied, but it was beside the point. He'd hired her to do a job — nothing more. Besides, she wasn't his type.

"Duncan," she said softly.

He looked at her and their eyes met. Hers were a deep blue, wide, with dark lashes. Her hair was different, he thought, remembering the curls. Tonight it was smooth, with waves. Sleek, he thought, although he preferred the curls. The dress was appropriate. He appreciated the way it emphasized her curves, not to mention the flash of thigh.

"You look good," he said.

She tugged at the hem of her dress. "It's Cameron's doing. He was great. Funny and really knowledgeable about fashion. He made a list of what shoes and evening bags go with each dress."

"Cameron knows his stuff."

"He mentioned you were college roommates."

Duncan chuckled. "That was a long time ago. I'll admit he was the first openly gay guy I'd ever met and that I wasn't happy to have him as my roommate."

"Too macho to understand?" she asked.

"Partially. I also had the idea that he would attack me in my sleep, which was pretty stupid of me. It took a while, but we became friends. When he moved back to L.A. a few years ago and opened his own business, he looked me up. I signed on as a client."

"He was nice," she said. "My cousins and Kami had a great time shopping, too."

"They went with you?"

"Uh-huh. You said I can keep the clothes, which is very nice of you, but honestly, can you see me wearing anything like this ever again? It's not exactly suitable for the classroom." She smiled. "So everyone came with me and offered opinions. As long as Cameron agreed with the choices, I got outfits they can wear later. We're all about the same size."

"You're going to give your cousins and their friend your clothes when this is done?"

"Isn't that okay? You said you didn't want them back."

"I don't have a lot of use for them. They're yours."

"Thank you."

He turned the idea over in his mind. He couldn't picture any other woman giving up an expensive wardrobe without a whole lot of motivation. Her comment about wearing them, or not wearing them, in the classroom made sense. But didn't she date? Didn't she want to hold on to them just because she could? The situation didn't make sense, which meant Duncan was going to have to figure it out. Success meant winning and winning meant understanding his opponent and exploiting his or her weakness. He might have bought Annie's time, but he didn't trust her. Not a big deal as he didn't trust anyone. Ever.

Annie ran her hands over the smooth leather of the seats. The car, an expensive German sedan, still smelled new. The engine was quiet, the dashboard filled with complex-looking displays. She had a feeling that an engineering degree would make working the stereo easier.

"Your car is really nice," she said. "Mine has this weird rattle in the dash. My mechanic says there's nothing wrong with how it drives, so I live with it. But it makes it tough to sing along with the radio."

"You can't get it fixed?"

She looked at him out of the corner of her eye. "I could," she said slowly. "And I will. Right after I win the lottery. But first I need new tires. It's always something, right? But that's okay. My car is really dependable. We have a deal — it starts for me every morning and I don't replace it."

His mouth twitched. "You talk to your car?"

"Sure. You probably don't."

"Your car and I have never met."

She laughed. "I can introduce you, if you'd like."

"No thanks." He turned left at the light.

"I've been thinking, we're going to have to tell people how we met. That's always the question right after 'How long have you been dating?' "

"Three months."

"Okay." She made a mental note. "How about saying it was Labor Day weekend. You were on your way to the beach when you saw me on the side of the road with a flat tire. You stopped to help."

"No one will believe that."

"You wouldn't stop?" She did her best not to sound disapproving. "You have to help people. It's good karma."

"Maybe I don't believe in karma."

"You don't have to — it still happens. I think the universe keeps the score pretty even."

"Doubtful. If that were true, I wouldn't be a success."

"Why not?"

"Haven't you read anything about me? I'm a total bastard. I hired you to prove otherwise."

"If you were a total bastard, you would have had Tim arrested the second you found out what he'd done. You were willing to let him pay back the money."

"Only because I didn't want the negative press." He glanced at her. "Be careful, Annie. Don't make the mistake of thinking I'm nicer than I am. You'll only get hurt."

Maybe. But didn't his warning her prove her point?

The hotel ballroom was large, elegant and extremely well-lit. Music from a suit-wearing combo drifted under the hum of conversation. Annie held on to her glass of club soda and lime and did her best not to look panicked. Well-dressed people chatted and laughed with each other. There were enough diamonds glittering to stretch from here to Montana. She had a feeling the cost of all the designer shoes would easily settle the national debt.

Duncan's world was an interesting place and about as far from her classroom as it was possible to get while staying on this planet. Still, she was here to do a job, so she remained by his side, smiling at him adoringly, endlessly shaking hands with people whose names she would never remember.

"How long have you and Duncan been dating?" a well-dressed woman in her forties asked.

"Three months," Annie said. "We met on Labor Day weekend."

"That's an eternity for our Duncan. You must be special."

"He's the special one," Annie said.

"You're not exactly his type."

Duncan must have heard. He put his arm around Annie and pulled her against him. "My type has changed."

"So I see."

Annie leaned into him, finding the closeness less awkward than she would have expected. Duncan was tall and well muscled. She could feel the power of him, but instead of making her nervous, his strength made her feel protected and safe. As if nothing bad could happen while he was around.

An illusion, she reminded herself. But a nice one.

When the woman moved away, Duncan led Annie over to another group of people and performed more introductions. One of the men there worked for a business magazine.

"Mind if I ask you a few questions?" he asked.

"No," she said. "As long as you don't mind me being nervous."

"Not into the press?"

"Not really."

"You can't date a guy like Duncan Patrick and expect to go unnoticed."

"So I've been told."

The man, slight and pale, in his mid-thirties asked, "How did you meet?"

She gave him the story about the Labor Day tire trouble. He didn't look convinced.

"Someone said you teach?"

"Kindergarten. I love working with kids. They're so excited about school. I know that it's up to me to keep that excitement alive, to prepare them to be successful in the education system. If we can show young children the thrill of learning, we can keep them in school through graduation and make sure they get to college."

The reporter blinked at her. "Okay. So why Duncan Patrick?"

She smiled. "Because he's a terrific guy. Although I have to tell you, the first thing I noticed was his laugh. He has a great laugh."

The reporter blinked again. "I've never

heard him laugh."

"Then I guess you're going to have to be more funny."

Duncan moved toward them. "Charles," he said, shaking the other man's hand. "Good to see you."

"You, too."

Duncan turned his attention to her. "Let's dance," he said, taking the glass from her and putting it on a tray by the wall. He grabbed her hand and led her from the reporter.

Annie waved at Charles, then tapped Duncan on the arm. "I don't really dance."

"It's not hard. I'll lead."

She didn't know if that would help. "Do you think we could convince everyone to play Duck, Duck, Goose instead? Because I'm really good at that."

Duncan stopped, turned to her and started to laugh. She was pleased to realize she hadn't lied about his laugh — it was great.

"You'll be fine," he said, pulling her into his arms.

"Okay, but I apologize in advance for stepping on your toes."

Despite the fact that he was taller, she fit easily against him. He moved with a sureness that made him easy to follow, guiding her with his body and the hand on her waist. After a few steps, she managed to relax a little.

He smelled good, she thought absently. Clean but masculine. His suit was soft under her fingers as she rested her hand on his shoulder. Heat enveloped her. Heat and something else. The whisper of a tingle low in her belly.

Annie kept moving on the outside, but on the inside, everything went still. Tingles? There weren't supposed to be any tingles. This was a job. She couldn't have *feelings* for Duncan Patrick. She shouldn't like him or be attracted to him. He was her boss and their time together was just for show.

Maybe it was just because she hadn't been on a date in so long, she told herself. It was like being really hungry. Any kind of food would make her stomach growl, even something she didn't really want. Duncan was a good-looking guy. Of course she would respond. But she was smart enough to be careful. This was kind of like a fairy tale. She was Cinderella and the ball would end at midnight. Or in her case, Christmas. Only, there wouldn't be a shoe to leave behind and in the end, no handsome prince would come after her.

■ ■ ■ ■

Annie held up better than he'd expected, Duncan thought two hours later. She'd managed to tell the story of his stopping to help her with her flat tire a dozen times. She was so enthused and sincere, even he was starting to believe her. The guests at the party seemed equally charmed and confused by Annie. He'd caught more than one questioning look, as if they were wondering what he was doing with someone so . . . nice.

Even Charles Patterson, a business reporter, had liked Annie. All Duncan needed was a couple of favorable articles to balance the negative ones.

He collected the drinks from the bartender and returned to Annie's side. He handed her the club soda with lime she'd requested — so far she hadn't had any alcohol — and bent toward her as she touched his arm.

"I was telling Charles that his information is wrong," she said to Duncan. "You're not closing a shipping facility in Indiana, are you?" Her eyes widened. "It's practically Christmas. Not only wouldn't you put people out of work for the holidays, but it's your busiest season. You need all the workers you can get."

She was half-right, Duncan thought grimly. This was his busy time, but he'd had every intention of closing the facility. The rural routes it served weren't profitable.

Annie stared at him, waiting for his response. He had a feeling she wasn't playing — that she actually believed he wouldn't want to put people out of work at Christmas. Charles looked smug, no doubt assuming the worst, which had always worked for him in the past.

Duncan swore silently and reminded himself that currently his reputation was more important than the bottom line.

"Annie's right," he said easily. "The facility is staying open at least through the first."

Charles raised his eyebrows. "Can I quote you on that?"

Duncan nodded.

"Interesting." The reporter moved away.

"Why would he think that about you?" she asked when they were alone. "No one would be that mean. It's Christmas." She took a sip of her drink. "It's my favorite time of year. In my family, we're big believers in more-is-more at the holidays." She laughed. "We always buy a really huge tree and then can't get it home, let alone in the house. Last year we had to cut off the top two feet, which is kind of sad. But they don't look that big on the lot. Then there's the decorating, the baking. I love Christmas carols. Jenny and Julie start to complain after a couple of days, but I keep playing them. Then we have Christmas movie-fest weekends when we watch all our favorites. What are some of your traditions?"

"I don't have any."

Her eyes widened. "Why not?"

"It's just a day, Annie."

"But it's Christmas. That makes it more than a day. It's about family and love and giving and imagining the best in the world."

"You're too naive. You need toughening up."

"And you need to spend some quality time listening to Christmas carols. Don't you decorate your house?"

He thought of his expensive condo and the look on his housekeeper's face if he dragged in a live tree to shed on the bamboo flooring.

"I usually travel for Christmas. Skiing or maybe somewhere warm."

"What about your family?"

"There's only my uncle and he does just fine without me."

She looked confused, as if he'd started speaking a foreign language. "Next you're going to tell me you don't exchange gifts."

"We don't."

She winced. "Tradition is important. Being together. It's special."

"Have you been a hopeless romantic your whole life?"

"Apparently. How long have you been a complete cynic?"

"Decades."

She surprised him by laughing. "At least you'll admit it. They say that's the first step in starting the healing process."

"There's nothing wrong with me."

"Want to take a survey of ten random people? I'll put my Christmas traditions up against your noncelebration and we'll see who falls on the side of normal."

"I don't need anyone else's opinion to tell me I'm right."

She grinned. "You don't have to go to the gym, do you? Carrying around that ego is enough of a workout."

"It keeps me in shape."

She laughed again. The sound made him smile. She was prettier than he'd first thought. Opinionated when she forgot to be shy. Loyal to the point of stupidity, at least when it came to her brother, but everyone had flaws. The answers she'd e-mailed earlier had given him facts about her life but hadn't told him much about who Annie really was. In a practical sense, she was what he'd needed — a nice girl. But she was also appealing in a lot of ways.

Without thinking, he leaned forward and pressed his mouth against hers. She stiffened slightly before relaxing into the kiss. Her mouth was soft and yielding. Aware of the people around them, he drew back. As he straightened, he heard the sound of her breath catch and caught the flash of surprise in her eyes. Then she blinked and it was gone.

"You didn't say anything about kissing," she whispered, her voice a little husky. "I think we're going to need a special clause to cover that."

"The kissing clause?"

She nodded. "Set limits early and reinforce them."

He chuckled. "I'm not one of your students."

"That doesn't mean you won't be getting a time-out."

# Four

Duncan arrived on time for his weekly lunch with his uncle. A tradition, he thought as he walked into the restaurant. Annie would be proud.

Lawrence was already there, sitting at their usual table, a Scotch in front of him. The older man waved him over.

"I didn't order you one," Lawrence said as he stood and the two men shook hands. "I know you don't drink during business hours."

They sat down. Duncan didn't bother with the menu. He had the same thing every week. The server brought him coffee, then left.

"Good job," Lawrence said, tapping the folded newspaper next to his place setting. "The article is positive. You said you wouldn't be closing the Indiana facility before Christmas. You can't change your mind now."

"I won't."

"The girl sounds interesting. What's her name?"

"Annie McCoy."

"Is she really a kindergarten teacher?"

"Yes. She's exactly who you told me to find. Nice, connected to her family, pretty and articulate."

"The reporter is smitten," Lawrence said and picked up his glass. "How long are you going to see her?"

"Until Christmas."

His uncle's gray eyes sharpened. "It's strictly business?"

Duncan thought about the brief kiss he and Annie had shared, then did his best to convince himself he'd only done it for show. "We're not dating, if that's what you're asking. I've hired her to do a job, nothing more."

"I'd like to meet her."

"You're too old for her."

His uncle grinned. "We'll let her be the judge of that."

They ordered lunch and talked business through the meal. On the way to his car, his cell phone rang. He looked at the screen — the number was unfamiliar.

"Yes?"

"Hi. It's Annie."

They had a business dinner to attend tomorrow night. "Is there a scheduling problem?"

"No. We're going to get our Christmas tree this afternoon and I thought you might want to come with us."

He stared at the phone a second before putting it back against his ear. "Why?"

He heard the smile in her voice as she spoke. "Because it's fun and you need a little Christmas in your life. No pressure. You don't have to if you don't want to."

Which he didn't. But instead of telling her that, he found himself asking, "What time?"

"Four. My house. I don't suppose you have a truck we could borrow? The tree never fits well on the top of my car."

"I have a fleet of trucks, Annie. That's what I do."

"Oh. Right. Could we borrow a little one? Nothing with more than four wheels."

He shifted the phone to the other ear. "This isn't about me at all, is it? You just wanted to borrow a truck."

"No. Well, the truck is a part of it, but I would have wanted you to come even if you'd said no to the truck."

"I'm not sure I believe that."

The humor fled her voice. "I won't lie to you, Duncan."

"I'll see you at four."

He hung up.

Women had lied to him before. A lot of them. They lied to get what they wanted. He would swear sometimes they lied for sport. Valentina had been the biggest liar of them all. She had told him she loved him and then she had left.

Annie changed out of her dress and low heels. She usually put on jeans after she got home from school, so there wasn't anything unusual about that. The difference was this time she wasn't just going to be hanging out at home. She would be seeing Duncan again and as much as she told herself it wasn't a big deal, she'd yet to be totally convinced.

To be honest, the man confused her. He'd bought her services as a pretend girlfriend to improve his reputation. Not exactly something that happened every day. She'd gone online and read several articles about him, which had proven he really was considered something of a bastard in the business world. But he'd also paid for an impressive party wardrobe, given Tim a second chance and he'd kissed her.

The kiss was actually the most startling event, but she didn't like to think about it too much. It had probably been for show, so everyone would think they really were together. A meaningless, practically sexless gesture. Well, for him. For her . . . there had been tingles.

Not like the tingles when they'd danced. Those had been in her chest, more about feeling safe and content than anything else. But the kissing tingles were completely different. They'd zipped and zinged all the way through her body, pausing in her breasts and between her legs. Those tingles had made her think about kissing him again and what Duncan would be like in bed.

Focus, she thought as she pulled on jeans. All the articles she'd read had talked about how he always got the details right. It was an excellent quality for a man to have in bed.

She didn't usually daydream about making love with a guy after a single date. Especially not a date that wasn't real. But something had happened when his mouth had briefly claimed hers. Something wonderful.

Now she reached for a red sweatshirt with Christmas geese marching across the front. Before putting it on, she wondered if she should wear something less boxy and more flattering. Something that would cause

Duncan to see her as a . . .

What? A woman? He already did. An actual girlfriend? Not likely. They were only pretend dating. She couldn't let herself forget that. Besides, two guys had already broken her heart. Was she going for a personal best by making it three?

She grabbed the sweatshirt and pulled it firmly over her head. She knew better, she reminded herself. The trick was going to be remembering that.

"We won't be decorating the tree tonight," Annie said as she sat next to Duncan in the cab of the truck he'd driven to her house. "The girls all have something they have to get to. A class or work. Besides, you're supposed to let the tree sit out in the garage for a couple of days before bringing it in."

"Why? It's not a puppy. It doesn't need to get used to being away from its mother."

She laughed. "I think it's about the branches settling. I have the tree stand set up in the garage, so we can put it in water as soon as we get it home."

Duncan had arrived right on time. Based on the suit he wore, he'd come from work.

"Did I take you away from something important?" she asked.

"Nothing that can't wait." He smiled. "My

assistant was surprised when I said I was leaving."

"Imagine what she'd think if she knew where you were actually going."

He chuckled.

She studied his profile. She liked the strength of his face, the chiseled jawline, the shape of his mouth. Her gaze lingered on the latter as she thought about him kissing her. Would he do it again? If he kissed her in a nonbusiness setting, then she would know for sure that he'd liked it as much as she had. Craziness, she told herself. She couldn't think about Duncan as anything but her boss. The hard part was that she wanted a husband and a family to love, but all she had was a bruised heart and a fear that no man was going to think of her as more than a friend.

They pulled into the Christmas-tree lot. Jenny, Julie and Kami were already there. Duncan parked next to Jenny's car.

"Brace yourself," Annie told him. "You're about to meet your match."

He raised his eyebrows. "I can handle it."

She grinned. "That's what every man thinks, right before he runs into trouble. You've been warned."

Annie watched Duncan get out of the truck and introduce himself to her cousins and Kami. By the time she reached them, the easy stuff was done.

"That article about you in last March's issue of *Time* was interesting," Julie said. "The press really hates you, huh?"

"A hazard of my occupation," Duncan said calmly.

"Except there are a lot of CEOs out there," Jenny pointed out. "They're not all hated. Although I'll give you the coverage of the purchase of the mobile home park wasn't fair. You offered the residents a fair deal and made sure they were taken care of."

"The thing is," Julie added, "If one person thinks you aren't nice, it's probably them. But if all the press people feel that way . . ."

"I'm misunderstood," Duncan said.

"Uh-huh." Jenny and Julie moved between him and Annie. Kami seemed more comfortable keeping out of the conversation.

"What is this, the Inquisition?" Annie joked, warmed by her cousins' protective questions but trying to lighten the mood. She might not have a husband and a baby, but she still had a family. She had to remember that.

"They have bright futures in the law."

"I'm not going to be a lawyer," Jenny said.

"But I am watching out for Annie. We all are."

Duncan did his best to look attentive rather than incredulous. Were these two college girls going to threaten him? They had neither the money nor the resources, and if it came to a battle of wills, he would leave them coughing in the dust.

None of which he said to them.

"I don't need that much defending," Annie said, looking uncomfortable. "Duncan, I'm sorry. I didn't know the twins were going to gang up on you this much."

"But a little would have been okay?"

"Sure."

He turned to the cousins. "Annie and I have a business arrangement. She'll be fine."

"You have to promise," one of the twins said. Duncan couldn't tell them apart.

"You have my word on it." Even if he and Annie didn't have an agreement, she wouldn't be at much risk. He didn't get involved enough for anyone to get their feelings hurt. Life was easier that way.

They went into the lot. The girls fanned out to look at trees, but Annie stayed by him.

"I'm sorry if they offended you," she began.

"Don't be. I respect them for thinking

they can take me."

She tilted her head. Blond curls tumbled to her shoulder. "No, you don't," she said slowly. "You think they're foolish."

"That, too."

"It's a family thing. We're a team. Like you and your uncle."

He and Lawrence were many things, but a team wasn't one of them. Duncan nodded because it was easier than having to explain. He watched Annie turn her attention to the rows of cut trees.

The air was thick with the smell of pine. There were a few shoppers talking over the sound of Christmas carols.

As Annie moved from tree to tree, he scanned the lot until he found the girls checking the price tag on a tree. Kami shook her head. The twins looked frustrated before moving to another tree. He turned back to Annie, who was gazing longingly at a tree that had to be fifteen feet, easy.

"You have eight-foot ceilings," he said, coming up behind her. "Learn from your past mistakes."

"Meaning we shouldn't buy something that won't fit." She sighed. "But it's beautiful." She glanced at the price tag. It was eighty-five dollars. "Maybe not."

"How much did you want to spend?" he asked.

"Under forty dollars. Less would be better. This is a family lot. They bring in the trees themselves. They cost a little more, but they're really fresh and it's kind of a tradition to come here."

"You're big on tradition, aren't you?"

"Uh-huh. The rhythm of life, year after year. It's fun."

He felt like Scrooge. The only thing he did year after year was count his money.

She stopped in front of another tree, then glanced at him. "Not too tall?"

"It looks like a great height."

She fingered the tag. It was sixty-five dollars. When she hesitated, he wanted to ask if twenty-five dollars really made that much difference. But he knew it did or Annie — the spokesperson for the wonders of Christmas — would cough up the money.

Duncan excused himself and found the owner of the lot. After a quiet conversation and the exchange of money, Duncan returned to Annie's side.

"Let's ask the guy if they have anything on sale," he said.

She looked at him pityingly. "Trees don't go on sale until a couple of days before Christmas."

"How can you be sure? Maybe there's a return or something."

"No one returns a Christmas tree."

He smiled. "And if you're wrong?"

She sighed. "Fine. I'll ask. But I'm telling you, there aren't any returns or seconds in the Christmas-tree business."

She looked around for the owner, then walked over to him. As Duncan watched, the man in the Santa T-shirt pointed to three different trees clustered together. Annie glanced at Duncan, then back at Santa guy.

"Seriously?" she was saying. "You have returns?"

"All the time. How high is your ceiling?"

"Eight feet." She turned to the girls, who had joined her. "Did you hear that? These are only thirty dollars."

They had a lengthy conversation about the merits of each tree. Finally one was chosen and put in the back of Duncan's truck. Annie watched anxiously as he tied it down, then she took her seat in the cab.

She waited until he climbed in next to her before touching his arm. "Thank you," she said quietly. "I don't know how much you paid him, and normally I wouldn't have accepted the gift. But it's Christmas and the girls love the tree. So thank you."

He started to say it wasn't him, then shrugged. "I need to get back to the office. You were taking too long, looking for a discount tree."

Her blue gaze never wavered. "You're not a bad guy. Why do you want people to think you are?"

"It's not about nice, it's about tough. Staying strong. That means making the hard decisions."

It also meant depending only on himself — the one person he could trust to be there for him. She might think connecting was everything, but he knew better.

"You don't have to be mean to be strong," she said.

"Sometimes you do," he told her and started the engine.

Annie had never paid attention to magazine articles on relaxation. Her life was busy — she didn't have time to become one with the moment. On her best day, she was only slightly behind. One her worst day, her to-do list stretched for miles. But now, as she sat in the elegant beachfront restaurant with Duncan's business associates and stared at the nine pieces of flatware around her place setting — most of which were totally foreign to her — she wished she'd at least read the paragraphs on how to breathe through panic.

She knew enough to start from outside and work her way in. There was also a fairly good chance that the horizontal three pieces above the decorative plate were for dessert. Or maybe dessert and cheese, and possibly coffee. The weird little fork could be for shrimp or even fish and the steak knife was clear, but what were the other three for?

Even more intimidating was the menu. While it was in English, there weren't any prices. Did that mean everything was priced à la carte? Or was there some jumbo total given out at the end of the meal? It wasn't that she was so worried about the price. Even the cost of a bowl of soup would probably make her faint. But she didn't want to order the most expensive thing on the menu by mistake.

She scanned the offerings again. There was a lobster tail, a market-price fish and Kobe beef. She was pretty sure if she avoided those, she would be fine. Her gaze lingered over the pasta dishes. Two of them were homemade ravioli. The twins would love that, she thought.

"You all right?" Duncan asked, leaning close. "You're looking tense about something."

"We couldn't have gone to a diner? Maybe ordered a burger?" she whispered, making him laugh.

The low chuckle seemed to move through her, making her aware of how close they sat and how great he looked in his dark suit. Duncan might be the meanest CEO two years running, but he sure could wear clothes.

"It's business," he told her. "This place is quiet."

"So is my McDonald's, anytime after eight."

One of the three waiters serving the table appeared at her elbow. "May I get you a cocktail?" he asked.

She hesitated, not sure what the best — make that appropriate — drink would be. Or should she wait for wine?

"Ever had a cosmopolitan?" Duncan asked.

"Like in *Sex in the City*? No, but I'd love to try one. Are they really pink?"

"Unfortunately," Duncan told her, then ordered Scotch for himself.

An older man sat down on the other side of Annie. She smiled at him as Duncan introduced him with the fact that Will Preston was the largest plumbing supply distributor on the West Coast.

"Nice to meet you," the man said as he sat down. "Do you work?"

"I'm a kindergarten teacher."

Will leaned toward her. "Then maybe you can answer a question for me. My wife loves to have the grandkids stay the night with us and they always want me to read them a story. It's not that I mind doing that, but they want the same story over and over again. I read it to them and they want to hear it again. Why is that?"

"Their brains aren't as developed as yours," she said. "They don't have the lifetime of experiences to draw on. So everything is new, all the time. A bedtime story offers the comfort of the familiar and they like that. They feel connected by the repetition, plus they probably hear something new every time. I would guess they also like having you read it to them, as well. Your voice, the way you pronounce the words, all become associated with time with you. You're making memories."

He frowned. "I hadn't thought about it like that." The frowned cleared. "Thank you, Annie. That makes me want to read to them more."

"I hope you will. Because thirty years from now, when they're reading to their children, they'll remember this time. It will always be something you've shared."

"Do you know what you want?" Duncan asked, reclaiming her attention.

She glanced at the menu. "I was thinking the twins would have enjoyed doggie bags from here."

She was about to say more when she caught Duncan's startled expression. Maybe talking about taking food home to her family wasn't a good thing, she thought, suddenly uncomfortable. She closed her menu and pressed her lips together.

"Annie here has some real insights into my grandkids," Will was telling the man across from him.

The man looked bored, although he nodded. Annie shifted in her seat.

Although she was dressed in one of the pretty cocktail dresses Cameron had picked out for her, she felt out of place. Everyone at the table was older and seemed to know each other. The women were laughing and talking with a casual ease that made her want to slowly back out of the room. Anywhere but here, she thought. What if she failed? What if Duncan decided she wasn't doing a good job? Would he change his mind about their deal? Would Tim be pulled out of rehab and sent to jail?

Stop it, she told herself. So what if everyone in this room had some impressive job and knew what all the forks were for? She was smart. She had a career she loved and she knew she made a difference. Duncan Patrick needed her to make himself look good. If anyone should be worried about the deal being changed, it was him, not her. He was lucky to have her.

"Do I want to know why you're smiling?" Duncan asked, leaning close and putting his arm on the back of her chair. "Are you drunk?"

"I've taken one sip."

"You don't seem like much of a drinker."

"Maybe not, but even I can handle a cocktail."

"Are you putting me in my place?"

"Do you need me to do that? I'm tougher than I look, Duncan."

He laughed. "I'm sure you are."

While it hadn't been her best time ever, Annie managed to get through the dinner without spilling, saying anything she regretted or withdrawing completely. She'd managed to hold her own on a debate about charter schools and had offered an opinion on the latest movie sensation. When everyone was standing up to leave, the waiter appeared with two large brown bags.

"For those hungry college girls you have at home," Duncan said. "Three entrées and dessert for all. It'll keep them out of your secret stash."

She was both surprised and touched. Talk about thoughtful. As they moved toward the exit, she walked slowly, waiting until everyone else had left. Then she put the bags on the nearby table, rested her hand on Duncan's shoulder, reached up and kissed him on the cheek.

"You're a total fraud," she whispered. "You're not mean at all."

He dropped his arm around her waist and drew her closer. When he kissed her back, it wasn't on the cheek and it wasn't meaningless. Duncan pressed his lips to hers with a force that took her breath away. He claimed, his mouth moving against hers. There was no doubt of what he wanted, or of the fact that his intensity hinted he might just take it without asking.

She was pressed against him, his arm like a band around her, holding her in place. There was no escape, but there also wasn't any fear, either. Instead of wanting to struggle with him, she found herself yielding, instinctively realizing that he expected a fight. Surrender was the only way to win.

As soon as she relaxed, so did his hold.

His mouth gentled, still taking but with a teasing quality. She was aware of silence around them, the air of expectation. He lightly brushed her bottom lip with his tongue.

Fire shot through her. She parted for him and he claimed her with a passion that left her weak. The second his tongue touched hers she was lost. Wanting poured through her, making her surge closer. Unfamiliar desperation swamped her. She wrapped her other arm around his neck and pressed harder against the thick muscles of his chest. He could snap her like a twig, if he wanted, and that was very much a part of his appeal. The strength of him. If Duncan ever fully committed to someone, that woman would be cared for and protected forever.

He stroked the inside of her mouth, exploring, arousing. She answered each touch with a brush of her own. His hands moved against her back, before dropping lower to her hips.

Heat invaded. Wanting grew. The need was unexpectedly powerful. She'd dated before, had made love before, had even thought she'd been in love before. But none of those experiences had prepared her for a passionate kiss in Duncan's arms.

Slowly, almost reluctantly, he drew back.

"Annie," he began, his tone warning.

She didn't know if he was going to remind her that their deal didn't include sex or that she was playing with fire. She met his dark, smoldering gaze and shook her head, then collected the doggie bags and turned to leave.

She didn't want to hear that she wasn't anyone he could be interested in. Not tonight. As to the danger of playing with fire . . . it was simply something she was going to have to risk.

# Five

"I'm sorry I can't make it tonight," Annie said, both frustrated and worried. She was starting to enjoy her evenings with Duncan at the various functions he took her to. But she was also worried about their deal. "I hope you understand. It's a holiday emergency."

"A contingency we seem to have missed in our agreement."

Annie couldn't tell if he was pissed or not and found herself a little nervous about asking.

"It's just we had a lot of no-shows last weekend when the parents were supposed to help with the set decorations."

"For the Christmas play?" he asked.

"It's a winter festival, Duncan. We don't promote any one holiday celebration."

"And calling it a winter festival fools people?"

She heard the humor in his voice. "It's

inclusive. So there are a bunch of sets to be built and painted. I have to stay and help."

"What is your class doing?"

"Singing 'Catch a Falling Star' while using American Sign Language at the same time."

"Multitasking at five. Impressive. All right, Ms. McCoy. Call me when the sets are decorated. If there's time, I'll take you to the cocktail party with me."

"I'm sorry to miss it," she said, sincere in her regret.

"You don't know that you will yet, do you?"

"We're not exactly a talented group when it comes to woodworking, Duncan. We're going to be here all night."

"Just call me."

She hung up and walked back into the main auditorium building. The other teachers and a couple of volunteers were dividing up the work. As the closest Annie had come to construction was the knitting class she'd taken the previous summer, she was given paint detail.

Thirty minutes later everyone was hard at work, building, sanding and painting. Fifteen minutes after that, four big guys in T-shirts, jeans and work boots walked in. Each man had an impressively large toolbox with him. The principal turned off the saw and removed her safety goggles.

"Can I help you?" she asked.

"We're here to help with the sets," one of the guys said. "Duncan Patrick sent us."

The teachers looked around in confusion. Annie cleared her throat. "He's, ah, a friend of mine. I mentioned we hadn't had our usual parent volunteers." She was trying to look perfectly normal, which probably wasn't working, seeing as she couldn't stop smiling. A light, happy feeling made her think she just might be able to float home instead of drive.

The principal sighed gratefully. "We are desperate. Have you ever worked on sets for a school play before?"

The men exchanged glances. "Two of us are cabinet makers, and two of us are house painters, ma'am. We can handle it. If you'll just tell us what needs to be done, leave us to finish it and we're good."

Annie pulled her cell phone out of her pocket and dialed Duncan's number. "Thank you," she whispered when he picked up. "This is amazing."

"This is me making sure you don't back out of our deal. I'll pick you up at five. It won't be a late evening."

She wanted to say more, to have him

admit he'd gone way out of his way to help her. But something inside her told her he didn't want to take credit for what he'd done. The question was why. What in Duncan's past made him believe that being nice and kind and honorable was a bad thing? Had someone hurt him? Maybe it was time to find out.

"I don't understand," Annie said as she put the key in the front door lock and turned it. "He's a banker. He has lots of money. So why does he care about yours?"

"Banks get money from other people and make profit off it," Duncan told her. "Loaning it out, investing it. The bigger the accounts, the more income for the bank."

"Okay," she said slowly, obviously not convinced.

They'd spent the past two hours at a boring cocktail party. In theory the evening had been about networking, but it had become clear that Duncan had been invited so a prominent banker could solicit his business. Normally he didn't mind being courted — it could make for an excellent deal. But tonight he hadn't been in the mood.

Instead he'd been watching the clock and checking his cell phone.

Annie shrugged out of her black wrap and

dropped it on the sofa. She bent over to remove her high heels, wincing as she pulled them off.

"They weren't kidding," she murmured, curling her toes into the carpet. "Beauty *is* pain."

Normally Duncan would have responded to the comment, but he was too busy watching her dress gape open, exposing her full, pale breasts. The curves looked big enough to fill his hands. Staring at them, he wondered how the soft skin would taste. He imagined his tongue circling her tight nipples, flicking them quickly as she writhed beneath him.

The image was vivid enough to cause blood to pool in his groin. He shifted uncomfortably.

Annie straightened, took a step and winced again. "I think the injury is permanent. How do women wear those shoes every day? I couldn't stand it." She pointed to the corner. "Isn't it beautiful?"

He glanced in that direction and saw the decorated Christmas tree by the window. It filled the space and spilled into the room. Hundreds of ornaments seemed to cover every inch of branch. Annie flipped on the lights, which flicked on and off at a dizzying speed. It wasn't something he would have liked and yet there was something special about the tree.

"Very nice."

"Did you get one yet for your place?" she asked.

Of course not, but he didn't want to hurt her feelings. Instead he pointed to the coffee table where an instruction manual lay inside a clear plastic sleeve. "What's that?"

She looked down, then picked up the package. "I don't know. It's for a freezer. We don't have a . . ."

Slowly she raised her head until she stared at him. "You didn't."

He pointed to the kitchen. Beyond that was a utility room with a washer, dryer and as of an hour ago, a brand-new freezer. She ran through the kitchen. He followed. When he'd caught up with her, she was running her hands lovingly down the door before opening it and gazing at the full shelves.

There were packages of meat, chicken and fish, a stack of frozen pizzas, bags of vegetables, containers of juice and ice cream. Annie stared for nearly a minute, her eyes wide, her mouth open. Then she closed the door and turned to face him.

He'd known a lot of beautiful women in his life. He'd slept with them, dated some, left more than a few. He'd been seduced by the best, even been married, but no one had looked at him the way she did now — tears in her blue eyes, a expression of pure happiness on her face.

"You didn't have to do that," she told him.

"I know. I wanted to. You can buy in bulk. It's cheaper. I know how you love a bargain."

"It's the best gift ever. Thank you." She reached for his hand and squeezed it. "Seriously, Duncan. This is life-changing."

He pulled back his hand, not wanting to be sucked into the moment. He'd seen a need and filled it. Big deal. "It's just a freezer."

"To you. To me it's something I don't have to worry about for a while. It's a chance to catch my breath."

He'd given gifts before. Jewelry. Cars. Vacations. Now, standing in Annie's shabby little house, he realized he'd never given anything that mattered. No one had been touched by something he'd done before. Maybe because Annie was one of the few women he'd ever liked.

Wanting and liking were completely different. He'd gone into this arrangement to improve his reputation and get his board of directors off his ass. But somewhere along the way, he'd started to like Annie. He couldn't tell if that was good or bad.

"This is my good deed for the holiday season," he said. "Don't read too much into it."

"Right." Her smile was knowing. "Because you're not a nice guy."

"I'm not."

"So I've heard." She pulled open the freezer again and removed a pizza. "This has everything on it. Does that work?"

"You're cooking a pizza?"

"They served only sushi at that cocktail party." She wrinkled her nose. "Raw fish isn't my favorite."

"Pizza it is."

She went back into the kitchen and started the oven. "Want to watch a Christmas movie while we wait?"

"No."

She laughed. "I'd let you pick which one."

"I'd still say no."

The tears were gone and now her eyes sparkled with laughter. "You're not overly domesticated, are you?"

"I never had a reason."

"But you were married. Didn't the former Mrs. Patrick tame you?"

He moved closer. "Do I look tamed?"

"Hmm." She squinted. "I think I can see

little marks on your cheeks where the reins went."

He reached for her and she ducked away. But she slipped on the vinyl floor. He caught her in his arms, her body yielding against his. The need to pull her close was strong, the desire instant. But the reminder of his ex killed the moment. He let her go.

"Valentina wasn't interested in domesticating me," he said, deliberately stepping back.

Annie leaned against the counter. "What was she like? Cameron said she was interesting."

"I doubt that. Cameron would have said she was a bitch."

"That, too."

Duncan didn't think about his ex-wife any more than he had to. "It was a long time ago," he said. "She was a journalism major in college. I'd just bought my first billion-dollar company. She came out to interview me for a paper she was writing. Or so she said. I think it was a way to meet me."

Valentina was four years younger than him, but she'd been cool, sophisticated and confident. He'd been a former boxer, over-muscled and accustomed to using his size to get his way. She was all about the subtle win.

"Is she beautiful?" Annie asked, not quite meeting his gaze.

"Yes. Blond hair, blue eyes." He studied the woman in front of him. Technically the description fit Annie as well, but the two women had nothing in common. Annie was soft and approachable. She trusted the world and thought the best of people. Valentina played to win and didn't care who got hurt in the process.

She'd smoothed his rough edges, had taught him what it meant to be a gentleman. Through her he'd learned about wine and the right clothes and which topics of conversation were safe for polite conversation. She was all about doing the right thing — until the bedroom door closed. There she preferred him as uncivilized as possible.

"How long were you married?"

"Three years."

"Did you . . ." Annie cleared her throat. "I assume you were in love with her. It wasn't a business arrangement."

"I loved her," he said curtly. As much as anyone could love a woman who kept her heart firmly protected in a case of ice. "Until I walked in on her screwing one of my business partners."

Not even in their bed, Duncan thought, still more angry than hurt at the memory.

On his desk.

"I threw her out and borrowed enough money to buy off all my partners," he said, looking past her but not seeing anything around them. Instead he saw a naked Valentina tossing her long hair over her shoulder.

"You weren't foolish enough to think I really loved you," she'd said in answer to his unspoken question.

He *had* been that foolish. All the time he'd been growing up he'd known he had to be strong to stay safe. With Valentina, he'd allowed himself to forget the painful lessons he learned in his youth. He never would again.

Annie touched his arm. "I'm sorry. I don't know why she would do something like that."

"Why, because in your world marriage is forever?"

"Of course." She looked shocked that he would even ask. "My dad died when I was really young. My mom talked about him all the time. She made him so real to me and Tim. It was like he wasn't dead — he'd just gone on a long trip. When she died, she told me not to be sad because when she was gone, she got to be with him again. That's what I want."

"It doesn't exist."

"Not every woman is like Valentina."

"You find anyone worthy of those dreams of yours?"

"No." She shrugged. "I keep falling for the wrong guy. I'm not sure why, but I'll figure it out."

She was optimistic beyond reason. "How many times have you had your heart broken?"

"Twice."

"What makes you think the next time will be different?"

"What makes you think it won't be?"

Because being in love meant being vulnerable. "You would give a guy *everything.* Only for him to use you for what he can get, then walk away? Life is a fight — better to win than lose."

"Are those the only two options?" she asked. "What happened to a win-win scenario? Don't they teach that in business school?"

"Maybe. But not in the school of hard knocks."

She reached for his hands and curled his fingers into fists. "It must have been frustrating to learn you couldn't use these to battle your way out of every situation."

"It was."

Annie hadn't known much about Duncan's ex-wife beyond what Cameron had told her. Now she had a clearer understanding of what had happened. Valentina had hurt Duncan more than he would admit. She'd broken his trust and battered his feelings. For a man who was used to using physical strength when backed into a corner, the situation had to have been devastating. He'd allowed himself to lead with his heart, only to have it beaten up and returned to him.

"There hasn't been anyone important since Valentina?" she asked, even though she already knew the answer.

"There have been those who tried," he said lightly.

"You're going to have to trust one of them. Don't you want a family?"

"I haven't decided."

She shook her head. "You have to admire the irony of life," she said. "I would love to find someone and settle down, have a houseful of kids and live happily ever after. The challenge is that I can't find anyone who sees me as the least bit interesting in the romantic department. You, on the other hand, have women throwing themselves at you, begging to be taken, but you're not interested." She stared into his gray eyes. "You shouldn't give up on love."

"I don't need your advice."

"I owe you something for the freezer."

"The pizza is enough."

"Okay. Want to go find something violent on television while I put this in the oven?"

"Sure."

She watched him walk out of the kitchen.

Knowing about his past explained a lot. What Duncan didn't realize was that under that tough exterior was a really nice guy, which he wouldn't want to hear anyway. Guys hated to be called nice. But he was. She couldn't turn around without tripping over the proof.

What had he been like before he'd met Valentina? A strong man, willing to trust and give his heart. Did it get any better than that? The oven beeped. She opened the pizza box, then slid the contents onto a cookie sheet and put it in the oven.

Did Duncan's ex have any regrets? Had she figured out everything she'd lost and wished for a second chance? Annie didn't know her, so she couldn't say. She only knew that if she were ever given a shot at a man like Duncan, she would hold on with both hands and never let go.

The office Christmas party was a complete disaster. Annie hated to be critical, but there was no escaping the uncomfortable silence, the uneasy glances being exchanged and the unnaturally loud bursts of laughter from nervous attendees. She could feel the fear of those around her. No one was eating or drinking, and nearly everyone kept checking the time as if desperate to make an escape.

"Interesting party," she murmured to Duncan as they stood by the main entrance to the hotel ballroom. While she thought it was nice Duncan wanted to greet everyone who attended, his presence wasn't helping the situation. He was big and powerful, which made relaxing even more difficult.

"These things are always tedious."

"Maybe if there'd been some music."

"Maybe." He looked over her head. "There's Jim in accounting. I need to go speak with him. I'll be right back."

She retreated to a private spot by a fake potted plant and called home. Jenny picked up on the first ring.

"Can you and Kami bring the karaoke machine?" she asked in a low voice. "I have a dead party that needs help." She gave the name of the hotel and which ballroom.

"Fancy," Jenny said.

"Disaster. Please hurry."

"We'll be there, Annie. Just keep sipping

the wine."

"I'm not sure it will help." She pushed the end button, then put her cell back in her purse.

Across the ballroom, Duncan talked to several men. Probably his executives, she thought, noticing how everyone else also kept their eyes on the group.

Three nights ago, he'd ended up leaving before the pizza was cooked, claiming he was going back to work. It was probably true, she told herself. Work was an escape. Not that she was anyone to complain. While she didn't work the crazy hours he did, she spent plenty of time avoiding what was wrong with her life. Her cousins and Kami kept her busy, not to mention all the projects through school and the various classes she'd signed up for. If she was constantly running, she didn't have to think about the fact that she hadn't been on a date in nearly six months. Not counting Duncan, of course.

After the holidays, she promised herself. She would get back out there and start dating. She would look for someone who saw her as more than a sister or a friend. Tim had offered to set her up with a couple of guys he knew. Although that had been before he'd gone into rehab. She wondered if her brother was still angry with her.

Because he wasn't able to get calls or have visitors for a couple more weeks, there was no way to know.

For the next twenty minutes, she sipped her wine and tried to talk to people at the party. They were all too tense to do more than say they were fine and yes, this was a great party. Just as nice as last year. Finally Jenny and Kami appeared with the karaoke machine and microphone.

"I put in songs from the eighties," Jenny said as she helped Kami set up the machine on a table by a plug. "I figured everyone here would be really old."

"Nice," Annie told her. "You're kidding, right?"

Jenny grinned. "You're so serious about everything. Yes, I'm kidding. There's mostly Christmas music loaded." She looked around at the dying party. "How are you going to get this started?"

Annie took another sip of wine. "I plan to sacrifice myself."

Kami winced. "Tim doesn't deserve you looking out for him the way you do."

"Tell me about it."

Annie nodded and Jenny flipped the switch. An electronic hum filled the room. Everyone turned to look. Annie waved weakly, then scrolled through the songs until she found "Jingle Bell Rock." Maybe that would put people in the holiday spirit.

The music came on. Kami turned it up, then mouthed, "Good luck."

Annie picked up the microphone and began to sing.

She had a modest voice, at best. Soft, without a lot of range. But someone had to save the party and everyone else was too afraid. So she did her best and ignored the waver in her voice and the heat burning her cheeks.

At the chorus, Jenny and Kami joined in. Then a couple of people in the crowd sang along. A few more sang the second chorus and by the third time around, most of the people in the room were nodding along.

A couple of women came up and said they wanted to sing. By the time they were done, there was a line of people waiting. She gratefully handed off the microphone.

She grabbed her wine and finished it in a single gulp. She was still shaking. The good news was people were actually talking to each other and she saw a couple filling plates with food.

Duncan joined her. "You were singing."

"I know."

His expression was hard to read. "Why?"

"Was it that bad?"

"No, but you were uncomfortable."

"The party was dying. Something had to be done."

Duncan looked around at his employees, then back at her. "This wasn't your responsibility."

"People should have a good time at an office party. Isn't that the point of giving it? So they can hang out together, talk and learn about each other in a way that isn't about work?"

He stared at her blankly.

She pointed at the people in the room. "Go talk to them. Ask questions about their lives. Pretend interest."

"Then what?"

"Smile. It will confuse them."

He looked at her quizzically, then did as she said. She watched him approach a group of guys who were drinking beer and tugging at their ties.

The employees weren't the only ones who were confused, she thought, staring at Duncan. She was, as well. She was with him for a reason that had nothing to do with caring or being involved. He'd basically blackmailed her into pretend dating him so he could fool the world into thinking he was a nice guy. So why did she want to be next to him now, helping him? Why did the sight of his smile make her want to smile in return?

Complications she couldn't afford, she reminded herself. She wanted forever and Duncan wanted to be left alone. She was staff, he was the boss. There were a thousand reasons why nothing would ever work out between them.

And not one of them could stop her from wishing for the very thing she could never have.

# Six

Duncan kept his hand firmly around Annie's elbow as he guided her toward his car in the parking lot. One of the first rules of boxing was not to fight mad. It gave your opponent an advantage. He'd learned the lesson also applied to all areas of life, so he wasn't going to say anything until he was sure he was under control. A state hard to imagine as anger pulsed in time with his heartbeat.

He was beyond pissed. He could feel the emotions boiling up inside him. The need to lash out, to yell — something he never did — nearly overwhelmed him.

"Just say it," Annie said calmly, when they reached the car.

He pushed the button to unlock the doors, then opened hers. "I have nothing to say."

She rolled her eyes. "You're practically frothing at the mouth. You need to just say it."

"I'm fine," he growled, waiting until she got into the car, then closing her door.

He walked around and got in on the driver's side. She put her hand on his arm.

"Duncan, you'll feel better."

He angled toward her, staring into her wide blue eyes, nearly vibrating with rage. "You had no right."

"So you *are* mad."

"What the hell were you thinking."

She sighed. "So much for the warm fuzzies."

He narrowed his gaze. "Excuse me?"

"Before, at the party, when I brought in the karaoke machine and humiliated myself by singing and saved the day, there were warm fuzzies. But now, all because I make a simple little suggestion, you're upset."

"A simple suggestion? Is that what you call it? You have no right. This isn't your business. Our bargain in no way gives you any kind of authority over me or my decisions. You don't know what you're talking about and because of that, I have to deal with your mess."

She nodded slowly. "Feel better?"

"I'm not a child to be placated."

"I'll take that as a no."

She wasn't afraid of him. In the back of his mind, he appreciated that she was sitting calmly while he ranted. Most people couldn't do that. They were too aware of his size, his background, his ability to physically rip them in two if the mood struck.

She shifted toward him. "It's not a bad idea."

"You're not the one who has to pay for it."

"You're paying for it already," she said reasonably. "Parents have to miss work because their day care isn't available. Or they can't stay late because of the hours. It's out of their control and that makes people worry. Worried people don't do as good a job."

"I'm not offering in-office day care. It's ridiculous."

"Why?"

"It's expensive and unnecessary."

"Do you know that for sure?" she asked.

"Do you know that it really helps?"

"No, but I'm willing to find out if it does. Are you?"

"I don't come into your classroom and tell you how to teach. I would appreciate it if you didn't come into my business and tell me how to run it." The anger bubbled again.

"I'm not doing that. I was talking to a group of your employees and they spoke pretty passionately about it. I said it was an interesting idea and something you'd look into."

"You do not speak for me."

"What was I supposed to do?" she asked, a slight edge to her voice. "As far as they're all concerned, I'm your girlfriend. The entire point of this exercise is to make the world think you're a nice guy. Nice guys listen to good ideas."

He couldn't take much more of this. "It's not a good idea. I listen when the person talking has something worthwhile to say."

"Oh, and I don't?" Now she was glaring. "Do I need an MBA to be worthy of a meeting? No wonder everyone was afraid to speak at that party. You don't allow them to communicate without your permission. Do they have to get it in writing in advance? Not listening to anyone else must make for short meetings. But why have a meeting at all? You're so damned all-knowing. That must make their jobs easier. You issue proclamations and they go forth and produce. What a concept."

She was seriously pissed. Her eyes flashed and color stained her cheeks. She actually leaned forward and poked him in his shoulder.

"Don't be a jerk," she said loudly. "You know this idea has merit. Other companies have put day care in place successfully. Maybe you're right — maybe it won't work, but the current system is causing problems. So fix it. Contract with a couple of day care places so they'll stay open later. Offer a program that allows employees to pay for day care with pretax dollars. I'm saying that if people who work for you think there's a problem, then there's a problem, whether you like it or not."

He leaned back against the door. "You about done?"

"No. The people at that party tonight were scared of you, Duncan. That's not a good thing."

He knew she was right about that. A frightened workforce put more energy into protecting themselves than into the company.

"I don't want them to be afraid," he admitted. "I want them to work hard."

"Most people can be motivated by a common goal a whole lot better than by intimidation."

"What intimidation? You're not scared of me."

"I don't work for you. Well, I guess I kind of do, but I know you. They don't. You can be a scary guy and you use that to your advantage. Maybe that was a successful strategy at one time, but now it's getting in your way."

"I'm not going to get all touchy-feely. I don't care about their feelings."

"Maybe not, but you don't have to be so obvious about it. You know I'm right about the day care problem. You should look into it."

She was right, dammit. Even more frustrating, he wasn't pissed anymore. How had she done that?

"You're a strange woman, Annie McCoy."

She smiled. "Part of my charm."

It was more than charm, he thought, reaching for her hand. He laced his fingers with hers, then pulled her close. She came willingly, leaning across the console. He stretched toward her, then pressed his mouth to hers.

Annie had never experienced makeup sex, but she'd heard it was terrific. If the fire shooting through her the second Duncan's lips touched hers was any indication of what it could be like, it was something she was going to have to look into.

Her body was energized from their argument. She'd enjoyed battling with him, knowing she could stand up for herself. While he could easily overpower her physically, emotionally they were on equal ground. And they would stay that way. A feeling in her gut told her Duncan fought fair.

She tilted her head, wanting more from the kiss. He tangled his free hand in her hair and parted his lips. She did the same, welcoming his tongue. He tasted of Scotch and mint. Heat from his body warmed her. She leaned closer and wrapped her arm around his neck.

They kissed deeply, straining toward each other. She ached inside — her breasts were swollen and there was a distinct pressure between her legs. If the car console hadn't been between them, she would have had a tough time keeping herself from pulling off his jacket and tearing off his shirt.

But instead of suggesting they take this somewhere else, he straightened, putting distance between them.

In the dark, she couldn't see his eyes and wasn't sure what he was thinking.

"You're a complication," he said at last.

Was that good or bad? "I'm also a Pisces who enjoys long walks on the beach and travel."

He laughed. As always, the sound made her stomach tighten.

"Dammit, Annie," he muttered before kissing her again. When he pulled back, he said, "I'm taking you home before we do something we'll both regret."

Regret? She had no plans for regrets. But not being sure of his response, she stayed silent. Wanting Duncan was one thing. Wanting Duncan and having him flat-out say he didn't want her back was more than she was willing to take on.

Courage was a tricky thing, she thought as she fastened her seat belt. Apparently she needed to work on hers.

Annie survived the next two parties fairly easily. She was getting the hang of meeting businesspeople and explaining that yes, she really did teach kindergarten and loved what she did. She'd made friends with a couple of the wives, which was nice, and had met several more business reporters. The world of the rich and successful was less intimidating than it had been at the beginning, as was Duncan himself. The only regret she felt was that he hadn't kissed her again.

She told herself it was probably for the best and in her best moments, she actually believed it. Duncan had made it more than clear that theirs was a business relationship. Anyone who didn't listen only had herself to blame if it all ended badly. She had been warned.

"What's in the box?" Duncan asked, after they'd left the marina hotel and were driving back toward her place.

She'd brought it out with her on the date and had told him she wouldn't discuss it until after the party.

"Christmas decorations," she said. "For your place. A small thank-you for all you've done."

He glanced at her. "What kind of decorations?" he asked, sounding suspicious.

"Nothing that will eat you in your sleep. They're pretty. You'll like them."

"Is that an opinion or a command?"

She grinned. "Maybe both."

"Fine," he said with a sigh. "Come on. I'll even let you put them where you think they should go."

Before she realized what he was doing, he'd gone north instead of south on the freeway. Fifteen minutes later, they pulled into underground parking at a high-rise condo building.

Annie told herself to stay calm. That his bringing her home didn't mean they'd gone from a fake couple to a real one. They were friends, nothing more. Friends who pretend dated. It happened all the time.

She followed him into the elevator where he pushed the button for the top floor. A penthouse, she thought, feeling her stomach flip over. She shouldn't be surprised.

The elevator opened onto a square landing. There were four condo doors. Duncan walked to the one on the left. He opened it and flipped on a light, then motioned for her to step inside.

The space was large and open, like the lofts she'd seen on the Home and Garden channel shows she liked. There were hardwood floors, a seating area in the middle, a flat-screen TV the size of a jumbo jet, windows with a view of Los Angeles and a kitchen off to the right. Her entire house, including the backyard, would easily fit just in what she could see. No doubt his place had more than one bathroom. Maybe she could send the twins over here to get ready on Friday nights. There would be a whole lot less screaming for the mirror at her place if she did.

Duncan closed the door, then glanced at her.

"It's nice," she said, taking in the neutral beige walls and taupe sofa. "Not a lot of color contrast."

"I like to keep things simple."

"Beige is the universal male color. Or so I've heard."

She followed him into the sitting area. Or

great room. She wasn't sure what it was called. The leather furniture looked comfortable enough and there were plenty of small tables. She put her purse on a chair and set the box on the table next to it. Duncan walked into the open kitchen.

"Want some wine?" he asked.

"Sure."

He looked back at her, his eyes bright with humor. "It's not in a box."

She laughed. "Lucky me."

While he poured, she brought out her decorations. There were three musical snow globes with different holiday settings. Two flameless candles that sat on painted bases. Some garland, a snowman liquid soap dispenser and a nativity scene. The last was still in the box, the small porcelain figures protected.

She glanced around the room. The candles and the garland could go on the dining table. The snow globes fit on the windowsill. Duncan didn't seem to have any blinds to get in the way. She spotted a hall bathroom and put the soap there, then set up the nativity display on the table under the massive TV. When she was done, Duncan handed her a glass of wine.

"Very nice," he said. "Homey."

"Are you lying?"

"No."

She couldn't tell if he meant it or not. "I wanted to bring a tree, but wasn't sure you were the type."

"My housekeeper would be unamused."

She wasn't surprised.

"Want to see the rest of the place?" he asked.

She looked around at the open room, the tall ceilings, and resisted the need to say "There's more?" Instead she nodded.

Next to the half bath she'd noticed was a guest room. It was bigger than any two bedrooms at her house, but that no longer surprised her. On the other side of the bath was a study. The walls were paneled, a big wood desk stood in the middle, but what caught her attention were the trophies on the built-in bookcases. There were dozens of them, some small, some large. A few were of boxing gloves, but most were figures of a man boxing.

"You won these," she said, not really asking a question.

He nodded and sipped his wine.

She crossed the carpeted floor to read a few of the engravings. Each trophy had his name. There were dates and locations. She also saw medals in glass cases.

"I don't get it," she said, facing him. "Why

do people want to hit each other?"

The corners of his mouth turned up. "It's not all about hitting. There's an art to it. A talent. You need power but also smarts. When to hit and where. You have to outthink your opponent. It's not all about size. Determination and experience play a part."

"Like in business," she said.

"The skill set translates."

She wrinkled her nose. "Doesn't it hurt when you get hit?"

"Some. But my uncle raised me. Boxing is what I knew. Without it, I would have just been some kid on the streets."

"You're saying hitting people kept you from being bad?"

"Something like that. Put down your glass."

She set it on the desk. He did the same, then stepped in front of her.

"Hit me," he said.

She tucked both hands behind her back. "I couldn't."

The amusement was back. "Do you actually think you can hurt me?"

She eyed his broad chest. "Probably not. And I might hurt myself."

He shrugged out of his suit jacket, then unfastened his tie. In one of those easy, sexy gestures, he pulled it free of his collar and tossed it over a chair.

"Raise your hands and make a fist," he said. "Thumbs out."

Feeling a little foolish, she did as he requested. He stood in front of her again, this time angled, his left side toward her.

"Hit me," he said. "Put your weight behind it. You can't hurt me."

"Are you challenging me?"

He grinned. "Think you can take me?"

Not on her best day, but she was willing to make the effort. She punched him in the arm. Not hard, but not lightly.

He frowned. "Anytime now."

"Funny."

"Try again. This time hit me like you mean it or I'll call you a girl."

"I *am* a girl."

She punched harder this time and felt the impact back to her shoulder. Duncan didn't even blink.

"Maybe I'd do better at tennis," she murmured.

"It's all about knowing what to do." He moved behind her and put his hands on her shoulders. "You want to bend your knees and keep your chin down. As you start the punch, think about a corkscrew." He demonstrated in slow motion.

"That will give you power," he said. "It's

a jab. A good jab can make a boxer's career. Lean into the punch."

She was sure his words were making sense, but it was difficult for her to think with him standing so close. She was aware of his body just inches from hers, of the strength and heat he radiated. There were so many responsibilities in her life, so many people depending on her. The need to simply relax into his arms was powerful.

Still, she did her best to pay attention, and when he stepped in front of her again so she could demonstrate, she did her best to remember what he'd said.

This time, she felt the impact all the way up her arm. There was a jarring sensation, but also the knowledge that she'd hit a lot harder.

"Did I bruise you?" she asked, almost hoping he would say yes, or at least rub his arm.

"No, but that was better. Did you feel the difference?"

"Yes, but I still wouldn't want to be a boxer."

"Probably for the best. You'd get your nose broken."

She dropped her arms to her sides. "I wouldn't want that." She leaned closer. "Have you had your nose broken?"

"A couple of times."

She peered at his handsome face. "I can't tell."

"I was lucky."

She put her hand on his chin to turn his head. He looked away, giving her a view of his profile. There was a small bump on his nose. Nothing she would have noticed.

"You couldn't just play tennis?" she asked.

He laughed, then captured her hand in his and faced her. They were standing close together, his fingers rubbing hers. She was aware of every part of him, of the way jolts of need moved up her arm to settle in other parts of her body.

The knees he'd told her to bend went a little weak. Her mouth went dry. She shivered slightly, but from cold. His eyes darkened slightly as he seemed to loom over her. For the first time in her life, she understood the statement "getting lost in his eyes."

His gaze dropped to her mouth. He swallowed.

"Annie."

The word was more breath than sound. She heard the wanting in his voice and felt an answering hunger burning inside her. There were a thousand reasons she should run and not a single reason to stay. She knew that she was the one at risk, knew that he wasn't looking for anything permanent. But the temptation was too great. Being around Duncan was the best part of her day.

He reached for her and she went willingly into his arms. He kissed her deeply, claiming her. She responded by parting her lips, wanting all that he offered. He slipped his tongue inside. She met him stroke for stroke, feeling the waves of shivers washing through her. Even as his mouth claimed hers, his hands were everywhere. Tracing the length of her spine, squeezing the curve of her butt, sliding up her hips to her waist.

There was a confidence to Duncan, a sureness that allowed her to relax. His strength made her want to surrender, because being around him was inherently safe.

She raised her hands to his shoulders, feeling the smoothness of his shirt against her palms. She brushed the back of his neck, then slid her fingers through his short dark hair. When he moved his hands up her sides, toward her breasts, she tensed in anticipation.

There was no fumbling, no hesitation. He cupped her curves in his palms, then used his thumb and forefinger to gently tease her tight nipples.

Sensations shot through her. As he brushed her nipples again and again, she found it difficult to breathe. She sucked on his tongue, then plunged into his mouth, taking as well as giving. She moved her hands up and down his back, feeling his strength. There were muscles everywhere. She supposed she could have been afraid, but she wasn't. Not of him.

He found the zipper to her dress and drew it down. She pulled back enough to shrug out of the short sleeves. The dress pooled at her feet. Wearing nothing but bikini panties and a low-cut bra, she gazed into his eyes. The fire there, the raw wanting, gave her courage. She looked lower and saw his erection.

Annie had always been a shy lover. She preferred the lights off and not a lot of talking. She hoped for the best and was understanding when the man in question seemed confused about what to do for her. She'd never found the act of making love anything other than . . . nice.

Watching Duncan's face tighten with need gave her a courage she hadn't realized she had. Holding his gaze with her own, she reached behind her and unfastened her bra. When it fell, a muscle in his cheek twitched. She reached for his hands, took them in hers, then brought them to her bare breasts.

The sensation of skin on skin made her

gasp. Even as he caressed the sensitive skin, he bent down and took one of her nipples in his mouth. He sucked deeply, pulling until she felt the answering tug between her thighs. He moved to the other breast.

Back and forth, licking and sucking, arousing her until every inch of her skin was on fire. She was ready to be taken, right there in the living room, on the sofa, the kitchen counter. At this point, she wasn't picky. Anything that would relieve the building pressure inside her.

As if reading her mind, Duncan moved a hand across her belly, then to the edge of her panties. He tugged at the elastic. The scrap of fabric fell and she stepped out of it.

Naked except for her shoes, she stood before him. She expected him to lead her to the bedroom. Instead he stunned her by dropping to his knees in front of her. He reached between her legs and gently parted her, then bent toward her and kissed her intimately.

It was a kiss unlike any other, she thought, her eyelids sinking closed as perfect pleasure swept through her. The hot, warm friction of his tongue on that one sensitive spot made her tremble. She had to hold on to his shoulder to keep from falling. Over and over he stroked her, licking that single place again and again.

The steady pace caused her to tense. He seemed to know exactly where and how often and just the right pressure. She had trouble breathing. She wanted to part her legs and press against him, but told herself to stay in control. Only, control seemed impossible.

Back and forth, back and forth, he moved his tongue against her. Her muscles tightened, she strained toward a heat, a force she couldn't understand and didn't want to stop. Her heart pounded in her chest. Then he slid one finger between her legs, pushing into her and rubbing her from the inside in perfect rhythm with his tongue.

Her climax exploded without warning. She opened her legs wider, wanting to feel all of it. The pleasure flooded her, making it difficult to stay standing. Her body shook and trembled, her legs threatened to give way. She called out his name and hung on as the pleasure slowly faded.

She'd barely found her way back to normal when he stood and swept her up in his arms. No one had carried her before, but she was too boneless to do anything but hang on.

He took her to the other side of the condo,

into a large master suite. Light spilled in from the hallway. She had a brief impression of a large bed, a fireplace and more tall windows, although these were covered. He lowered her to the bed.

Somewhere along the way, she'd lost her shoes. Naked, she sat up to watch him quickly undress. When he pulled off his shirt, she saw the muscles she'd only felt before. He was as big and powerful as she'd imagined. He kicked off his shoes, pulled off his socks, then removed his pants and briefs in one quick movement.

His erection was impressive and a little scary. He pulled a box of condoms out of the dresser drawer, then slid next to her on the bed. But instead of going into his arms, she sat up so she could look at him. She put a hand on his chest and felt the sculpted muscles there. She traced the length of his thigh, smiling as his arousal jumped slightly as she moved by without touching. She explored the hair angling down his belly and ran her fingers along the outline of his six-pack.

Once again she was aware of his physical power. That he could crush her without breaking a sweat. She looked into his eyes, then reached for his erection and stroked the length of him. His mouth curved in a satisfied male smile.

"Want to be on top?" he asked.

"Next time."

What she really wanted was to feel him over her, moving in her. She wanted to run her fingers across his shoulders and arms, reveling in the force and power of him.

Without warning, he shifted. Suddenly he was kneeling over her and she was on her back. He put on the condom, then eased open her thighs.

She reached down to guide him in. He pushed into her, moving slowly, steadily, stretching her, filling her until the pressure was beyond exquisite. He braced himself and thrust in her again.

She lost herself in the sensation of him inside her. She gave herself over to their lovemaking, wrapping her legs around his hips and hanging on for the ride. Happy nerve endings came to life again. She'd wanted to watch his face as he got closer, but found her eyes slipping closed as the pleasure filled her, taking her beyond where she'd ever been before.

# SEVEN

Duncan stood by the coffeemaker. He'd already showered and dressed. On a normal morning, he would have left for work by now. But nothing about this morning was normal.

Annie had spent the night.

There were several problems with that statement. Usually he preferred to be at the woman's place so he could control when he left. But between the twins, Kami and what he would guess was a small, girly bedroom, his place made more sense. There was also the fact that last night hadn't exactly been planned. When he and Annie had set up their deal, he'd promised her he wasn't interested in sex. Apparently he'd been lying.

While making love with her had been pretty damned great, he was concerned about what happened next. Annie wasn't like his usual women, nor was she the affair type. Would she read too much into what had happened between them? Would she expect things? He also didn't want her to get hurt.

He heard footsteps in the hall. She walked into the kitchen, wearing the same cocktail dress she'd had on the night before. Her hair was still damp from the shower, her face free of makeup. She looked pretty and innocent and not at all the woman who had surrendered so passionately just a few hours before.

"You're looking tense," she said as she picked up one of the mugs he'd left on the counter and poured coffee. "Afraid I'm expecting a proposal?"

Shocked, he quickly said, "No." Proposal? As in . . .

She smiled. "I was thinking that a simple ceremony would be best, under the circumstances. The twins and Kami will want to be bridesmaids, of course."

He'd thought she might be confused or upset or even embarrassed. He'd been wrong on all three counts. It had been a long time since a woman had surprised him in a good way.

He crossed to her and took her free hand in his. "Will you wear white, my darling?"

She sighed. "I was trying to make you

nervous."

"I was playing along."

"You were supposed to be scared."

He kissed her. "Maybe next time." He released her hand.

"You're too in control of every situation," she complained, then sipped her coffee. "While you were snoring away, I had to stumble through a conversation with Jenny, trying to explain why I wasn't coming home without mentioning the fact that we'd had sex."

He looked at her. "Why would she have to know anything?"

"Because everyone would have noticed my empty bed and been worried."

"Life is easier without family."

"You're too cynical. One phone call is a small price to pay for having the girls in my life and don't pretend you don't understand that."

He did understand but didn't agree the price was worth it.

She smiled. "Now you have the thrill of them knowing about your sex life."

Something he could have lived without. Not that he didn't like the girls, but didn't this fall under the category of too much information? "Tell me they didn't ask any questions," he muttered.

"Only if you'd used a condom."

Annie kept her chin high as she spoke, but he saw the flush on her cheeks. She was an interesting combination of shy and determined, bossy and yielding.

"What did you say?"

She cleared her throat. "I said you had. . . . All three times."

He held in a grin. "And?"

"Jenny hung up."

They laughed together.

Annie looked good in the morning light. The riot of still-damp curls seemed to glow, like a halo. Her mouth was full, her cheeks still pink. Hers was a quiet beauty, he thought. One that would age well. She would be even more striking in her fifties. If he'd met her before he'd met Valentina, he would have been intrigued by the possibilities. Or maybe not. Maybe the appeal of the bad girl would have been too strong. Maybe he'd needed to be burned to learn his lesson.

And learn it he had. Trust no one. Don't give away anything for free and never, under any circumstances, risk his heart.

"You know this can't be more than it is," he said flatly.

Annie sipped her coffee, then drew in a breath. "Is that your way of saying not to get my hopes up? That this is simply a business arrangement with benefits?"

"Something like that." Too late he remembered he'd promised that sex had no part in their bargain. "When the holiday season ends, so do we."

"I've never had a relationship with an expiration date," she said, staring into his eyes, a faint smile on her lips. "It's okay, Duncan. I know the rules and I won't try to change them."

"I'm not sure I believe you. You're a happy-ending kind of woman."

"It's what I want," she admitted. "I want to find someone I can love and respect. A man who wants desperately to be with me. I want kids and a dog and some hamsters. But that's not you, is it?"

"No."

Years ago, maybe. Now, the price was too high. Getting involved meant putting too much on the line. He only played to win and in marriage, there was no guarantee. Valentina had taught him that, as well.

"You weren't supposed to sleep with me," she said.

"I know." He couldn't figure out her mood. Was she teasing or pissed? "Do you want me to apologize?"

She drew in a breath. "No. I want you to

promise that when this is over, you won't tell me you want to be friends. It will just be over. You have to promise."

"We won't be friends," he said, and then felt an odd sense of loss at the words. Annie was one of the few people he liked. He would miss her. But he *would* let her go.

Annie spent the day trying not to grin like an idiot. She wasn't worried her students would notice, but her fellow teachers certainly would. Then they would start to ask questions and she wasn't that good a liar. Probably a good quality, she told herself as she drove into her driveway and got out of the car. Under normal circumstances.

As she walked to the mailbox, she felt the lingering soreness in her legs and hips. Muscles not used to being stretched and used complained a little. Not that she minded. It was a good kind of ache — one that reminded her what had happened the night before. In Duncan's bed.

No regrets, she'd promised herself and that was how she felt. No regrets. Being with him had been spectacular. Her body had done things she hadn't known were possible. The time in his arms had shown her what she wanted in her life. Not just a great love, but also great passion. With the two other men, she'd been settling. She hadn't realized it at the time, but it was true. She would never settle again.

"Big words for someone who isn't even dating," she murmured, picking up the envelopes and flipping through them. "Well, not real dating." No matter how much she wanted him to, Duncan didn't count.

She reached the last envelope and winced. It was from the college, probably reminding her that tuition had to be paid. As she opened the envelope, she thought about her sad little bank account and wondered where she was going to find the money. Everything was so expensive. Maybe after the holidays she should get serious about finding a second job. One that . . .

Annie stared at the single sheet of paper. The one that said the tuition had been paid for for the rest of the year. Not just the quarter but the year. Paid in full.

Just looking at the total made her feel queasy. But the big "Paid" next to it wasn't possible. She hadn't and it wasn't as if Jenny had suddenly come into a bunch of money.

Annie walked into the house and looked through the mail again. There was also an envelope from Julie's college. The letter said the same thing. Tuition was paid for for the rest of the year. In full.

The shock made sense. The information, not to mention the action required, was unexpected. Before last night she might have been a little upset but more grateful. Now she felt all twisted up inside. Confused and slightly tarnished.

Dropping the rest of the mail, she returned to her car. The drive to Duncan's office wasn't far. His shipping empire was run out of a huge complex of buildings close to the Port of Los Angeles. She gave her name to the guard at the gate and had to wait while a series of calls were made. Finally she was given a visitor's parking permit and directions to where she should park.

She passed large warehouses and eighteen-wheelers waiting to be loaded. There were dozens of people walking and driving in every direction. Following the signs that pointed to the corporate offices, she managed to find the visitors' parking spaces and make her way into the six-story building.

It was an empire and a half, she thought as she stood in the lobby of Patrick Industries. A huge lit board showed a world map. Thousands of lights indicated the location of various company vehicles. Little icons indicated trucks, railcars and ships.

Annie had always known Duncan was a rich, powerful man. But those were just words. They hadn't been real. An intellectual understanding wasn't the same as looking at that map and seeing how incredibly successful he was.

She tugged at the sleeve of her oversize sweater, aware that the Christmas elves dancing across the front and back of it were great for a kindergarten classroom but a little out of place in corporate America. There was a big paint stain on her skirt and the back was wrinkled from the time she'd spent sitting on the floor while reading to her students.

"Ms. McCoy?"

Annie turned toward the speaker. A well-dressed woman in her thirties smiled.

"Mr. Patrick is expecting you. If you'll follow me, please."

Annie nodded.

They took the elevator to the sixth floor and stepped out onto a quiet floor of conference rooms and offices. People in suits moved purposefully, barely glancing at her. She followed the woman to an open double door. Inside, a middle-aged woman nodded.

"You can go right in."

Annie stared at the tall, wood door in front of her. It looked heavy and impressive. Unexpected nerves danced in her stomach.

Still clutching the letters from the colleges, she opened the door and walked into Duncan's office.

The space was even larger than his condo. Big windows overlooked the shipping yard on one side and the lobby on the other. Apparently this particular king enjoyed looking at his empire.

His desk was practically big enough for a plane to land on. There was a grouping of sofas in one corner and a conference table in another.

The man himself sat looking at a computer screen. He tapped a few keys, then glanced at her and raised his eyebrows.

"An unexpected pleasure," he said as he stood and walked around the desk.

He looked good. Too good. She'd seen him in his tailored suits before, so that wasn't anything she couldn't handle. Maybe the problem was less than twelve hours ago, she'd been in his bed and they'd both been naked. They'd slept in a tangle of legs and arms, only to awaken and make love again.

He stopped in front of her. "Everything all right?" he asked. "You look pale. Don't you feel well?"

Apparently unable to speak, she thrust the letters at him, then managed to find her voice. "You did this, didn't you? I won't even ask how you got the information to make the payments. It was the twins, wasn't it? You talked to them."

One corner of his mouth curved up. "I thought you weren't going to ask."

She shook the papers. "This isn't funny. You can't go around doing this."

"Helping people? I would have thought you would approve. Aren't you the one who told me it would be easier to actually *be* nice than to hire you and pretend?"

"What?" She dropped her arm to her side. "Duncan, why did you do this?"

"Because I could. Are you the only one who gets to be nice?"

"Don't be reasonable." She was tired from lack of sleep and felt the beginnings of a headache. "It makes me uncomfortable."

His smile faded. "That's not what I wanted. It's just a check, Annie. Don't make it into anything else."

"A big check. Two big checks." She glanced around to make sure they were alone, then lowered her voice. "We had sex. You can't buy me stuff."

The humor returned. "Most women would tell you the opposite. That after sex is when the buying begins."

"Maybe. If we were dating. But we're not. We have an arrangement. A deal. This isn't part of the deal."

"You're complaining because I'm giving you more?"

No. She was worried that if he was nice, if he was approachable and kind, she wouldn't have a chance of getting out of this with her heart in one piece.

The truth slammed into her and it was all she could do to stay standing. Of course. Why hadn't she realized it before? Duncan was a force of nature and she was just a regular person. He was rich and strong and powerful and unlike anyone she'd ever known. She'd been in trouble from the second they'd met.

"I . . ." She swallowed. "You didn't have to do this."

"I wanted to."

"It will make things a lot easier. Thank you."

He moved close and cupped her face in his large hands. "Was that so hard?"

"No."

He was going to kiss her and she was going to let him. It was already too late to try to protect herself. The best she could do was see this to the end and pray she wasn't totally devastated when it was over. A test of strength, she thought. A trial by fire.

His mouth moved against hers in a way

that had become familiar. There was always the taking, but it was tempered somehow. Maybe by her own hunger, her need for him.

She released the papers and let them fall to the floor so she could wrap her arms around his neck. He drew her against him and she went willingly. The kiss deepened. Passion swept through her. Now, she thought, burning with hunger. She wanted him now.

She squirmed to get closer and felt his arousal, thick and hard against her belly. It would be so easy, right here on his big desk. The one in the room with all the windows. Where anyone could see or walk in.

He drew back and looked into her eyes. "Reality check."

She nodded. "There are a lot of people all around."

"At the time, the windows seemed like a good idea."

Now it was her turn to smile. "And today?"

"Not so good."

He kissed her again, more lightly this time. Then he released her.

She stepped away reluctantly. He picked up the papers she'd dropped and handed them to her.

She folded them and put them in her purse. "Thank you for doing this. It really helps."

"You're welcome." He put his arm around her and guided her to the door. "My uncle Lawrence wants to meet you."

"I'd like to meet him, too." she said. Maybe find a moment to ask what Duncan had been like when he'd been younger.

"How about Sunday for dinner? My place?"

"I'd like that."

She'd like a lot more, she thought as she made her way back to her car. A chance to make this all real. A foolish wish, she reminded herself. Duncan had been clear about what he wanted from the beginning. From all that she knew, he wasn't the kind of man who changed his mind about anything.

After Annie left, Duncan found it difficult to refocus on work. The report on his computer was a lot less interesting than it had been before she'd stopped by. He found himself wanting to go after her. Maybe take her to his place for the rest of the afternoon . . . and the evening. But he had meetings and something inside him warned him that he would have to be careful. He didn't want her reading too much into their relationship. He appreciated all that Annie had done and didn't want her getting hurt.

At four, his assistant buzzed to tell him a Ms. Morgan had arrived for their meeting. Duncan glanced at his calendar, then frowned as he couldn't place the name. Someone from accounting, the note said.

"Send her in."

Seconds later a short, fifty-something woman walked in and smiled shyly. She wore her hair short and had on a drab suit and sensible shoes.

"Ms. Morgan," he said, pointing to the chair on the other side of his desk.

"Thank you for seeing me, Mr. Patrick."

The woman had a folder in her hands. She looked both determined and nervous.

When she was seated, he offered her coffee, which she refused. She cleared her throat.

"I talked to Annie at the Christmas party," she began. "She's very nice and when I mentioned I had some ideas about making a few changes, she encouraged me to come talk to you."

Typical, he thought, both annoyed and unsurprised. "Annie is a big believer in communication," he said shortly.

Ms. Morgan swallowed. "Yes, well, I

thought about what she said and decided to make the appointment. I'm a CPA, Mr. Patrick. I wasn't sure if you knew that. I'm required to take continuing education every year. I recently attended a class on depreciation."

"Rather you than me," he murmured.

She flashed him a smile. "It was more interesting than it sounds. There have been several changes in the tax code that could have a big impact on the bottom line. If I could just show you."

She opened the folder and passed over several pages. They went over them, line by line, as she explained how they weren't taking advantage of new classifications and schedules. The small changes were significant when applied to his large fleet of trucks.

"The tax savings alone is well into the high six figures," she said twenty minutes later.

"Impressive. Thank you, Ms. Morgan. I appreciate you bringing this to my attention. I'll speak to the vice president of finance and make sure these changes are implemented."

His employee beamed. "I'm happy to help."

She was. He could see it in her pleased expression. He'd always been one to manage through fear and intimidation. He'd never nurtured anyone, preferring to do it himself rather than be part of a team. Growing the company had required him to change his style. Entrepreneurs either learned how to work in a large organization or their companies stayed small.

But while Duncan had learned the lesson, he'd never liked it. Now, watching Ms. Morgan gather up her papers, he saw the benefit of encouragement. Maybe Annie was right. Maybe he should talk to his employees more. Trust them to do the right thing. Reward good behavior. What was it she'd told him? Set limits and reinforce them often.

"You'll be getting a check for ten percent of the savings," he said.

Ms. Morgan blinked at him. "Excuse me?"

"You're saving the company a lot of money. I appreciate that. You'll share in the benefit. It's a new policy. I want to encourage people to offer suggestions that either grow the business or save us money. If we implement the idea, that employee gets ten percent of the increase in sales or the savings."

The color drained from her face. "But ten percent of that amount is nearly my year's salary."

He shrugged. "That makes it a good day."

She opened her mouth, then closed it. "You're sure?"

He nodded.

"Thank you, Mr. Patrick. I'm — I don't know what to say. Thank you. Thank you."

She rose and hurried out. By the time she got to the door, he was pretty sure she was crying.

When he was alone, Duncan leaned back in his chair. He felt good — like he'd done the right thing. Maybe it was possible to find the occasional win–win scenario, he thought as he turned back to his computer. He began to type an e-mail to his chief operating officer, explaining the new policy of giving employees ten percent of saving or sales increases. Maybe someone in PR could leak the memo to the press. That should go a long way to getting him off the meanest CEO list.

After that, he would move forward with his plan to buy out his board and run the company himself. The way he liked — answering to no one. Although he would keep the new policy. Not for Annie, he told himself. He'd keep it because it made business sense.

# EIGHT

Annie knocked on Duncan's front door. She was more nervous than she had been before their first date, but this anxiety had nothing to do with Duncan. Instead she was about to meet his only living family member — Lawrence Patrick — and she desperately wanted the older man to like her.

She'd brought a Bundt cake and two DVDs, but wasn't sure about either. Maybe she should have brought her cousins or Kami to be a distraction.

The door opened and she saw a tall, handsome, older man with graying hair and eyes that were exactly like Duncan's.

"You must be Annie," the gentleman said. "Come in, come in. I've been waiting to meet you, but Duncan has insisted on keeping you all to himself. Probably because he knows I have a way with the ladies." Lawrence winked at her, then gave her a warm smile that melted away her nervousness.

He took the cake container from her and sniffed. "Do I smell chocolate? My favorite."

"I'm glad. It's lovely to finally meet you," she said, closing the door behind her.

"And you, young lady. I'm hearing very good things about you. My nephew isn't one to speak well of others, so you must be something special."

Duncan strolled toward them. "Come on, Lawrence," he said with a resigned sigh. "Let's wait at least ten minutes before you go telling Annie all of my flaws."

His uncle chuckled. "All right, but no longer." He turned to Annie. "Duncan has a teleconference with China in a few minutes. We'll have plenty of time to get to know each other while he's tied up."

"I look forward to it," she said.

"Great," Duncan muttered, but there was humor lurking in his gray eyes and he pulled her close for a brief kiss. "Don't fall for the old guy's charm. He's had decades of practice with the ladies."

She laughed. "Maybe I like a man who knows what he's doing."

"Sassy," Lawrence said. "I like that."

They went into the great room. Annie pulled out one of the DVDs she'd brought. "I saw this and couldn't resist."

Lawrence stared at the cover, then started

laughing.

Duncan shook his head. "You're encouraging him."

Annie set the copy of the movie *Rocky* on the coffee table and settled on the sofa across from Lawrence. The older man took a comfortable chair, while Duncan sat next to her.

"Rocky was a southpaw," Lawrence told her. "Left handed. They're a special breed. A lot of fighters don't want anything to do with them. They can't adjust. A great boxer knows how to think, how to anticipate."

Duncan stood. "I'm going to get ready for my call. Feel free to doze off, Annie. Lawrence loves to talk."

"I'll be telling her your secrets," Lawrence said.

"I have no doubt."

Duncan went into his study. Lawrence barely waited for the door to close before saying, "I know about the deal you have with Duncan. Why you're helping him."

"Oh." She hadn't been expecting him to say that. "My brother has some problems. This seemed the only way to get him help."

"I'm not saying it's a bad thing. But you're not acting like someone doing a job. Are you that good an actress?"

She looked down at her lap, then back at

him. "No. I'm not. I like Duncan. He can seem really hard and distant, but I don't think that's who he is. There's kindness in him. He's a good man."

Lawrence nodded slowly. "Not too many people see that side of him. They believe the press. It takes strength to take a failing business and grow it into an empire. He did that. He fought his way out of his circumstances."

Circumstances Annie didn't know much about. "I know you helped raise him," she said.

"The blind leading the blind," Lawrence told her. "My sister was a flake. She was a lot younger than me — a surprise baby. Our parents were so happy to have another child. They adored her. She was spoiled, always getting her way. After they died, she took her half of the money and disappeared. A couple years later, she came back pregnant. Wouldn't say who the father was. I'm not sure she knew. She had Duncan, then took off again. That's how it was, the first dozen or so years of his life. She would come and go. It broke his heart."

Annie looked at the closed study door and wondered about the little boy who had been abandoned over and over by his mother.

"When Duncan was eleven or twelve, he

told his mother to either stay or go. She had to pick. I think he was hoping she would choose to be a part of his life. Instead she disappeared. He never mentioned her again. I got word a few years later that she'd died. I told him. He said it didn't matter."

Hiding the pain, she thought sadly. Because it had to have mattered. First his mother had betrayed him, then Valentina had. Duncan had learned difficult lessons from the women who were supposed to love him. No wonder he didn't let anyone inside.

"I was hard on him," Lawrence admitted. "I didn't know anything about raising a kid. I took him to the gym with me, taught him to box. He was set on college, which confused the hell out of me, but he made it. Got a scholarship and everything." There was pride in his voice.

"He's a good man, and a lot of that is because of you," she said.

"I hope so. You know about his ex-wife?"

She nodded.

"There was a disaster. I never liked her and I'm glad she's gone, but now I worry Duncan won't ever settle down. He needs a family. Someone to come home to."

Not a very subtle message, Annie thought, wishing it were a possibility. "Duncan was very clear," she said. "This is a business relationship, nothing more."

"Is that what you want?"

A simple question with an easy answer. "I'm not the only one who gets to decide."

"Maybe not, but you can influence him."

"You're giving me too much credit."

"You'd be surprised."

If only, she thought. After all he'd been through, she wasn't sure Duncan would ever be willing to give his heart and she couldn't settle for anything less.

"I hope he finds someone," she said.

"Even if that means someone other than you?"

"Of course."

Lawrence stared at her for a long time. "You know what? I believe you. Which makes me hope things work out. Don't give up on my nephew, Annie. He's not easy, but he's worth it."

Before she could say anything in response, the study door opened and Duncan came out.

"You about done telling her all my secrets?" he asked his uncle."

"No, but we made a good start at it."

Duncan chuckled. "Glad I could help. Ready to watch the movie?"

"Sure." Lawrence winked at her. "While he's playing with his electronics, let me tell you about the time I beat a southpaw. It was back in '72. Miami. Talk about a hot day."

Duncan groaned, putting the DVD into the player.

"I don't mind," Annie said honestly. "Were you the favorite?"

Lawrence grinned. "Honey, I was practically a god."

Annie shelved her heart-to-heart with Lawrence as her commitments with Duncan took center stage. The following Monday, she attended a party at an art gallery that featured stark modern paintings that were beyond confusing. The single tiny red dot on the snow-white canvas was the least of the strangeness. There was a collection of black paintings. Just black. Apparently they were supposed to represent bleakness, and as far as she was concerned, the artist had done a fine job.

Wednesday night was a charity fund-raiser with an auction of ornaments painted by celebrities. Duncan bought a beautiful tree done by Dolly Parton. For Lawrence, he claimed, but Annie wondered if he might have a little crush on the singer himself. Tonight was a dinner at the Getty Museum in Malibu. Duncan was picking her up at five, which meant she had to be home no later than four so she could get ready. She was nearly on time, a positive sign. Then she felt the telltale uneven thudding that signaled another flat tire.

"No!" Annie yelled, slapping her steering wheel. "Not tonight. It's not a good time." Although she couldn't think when a better time might be. She was always running somewhere.

She pulled into a mini-mart parking lot and got out of her car. The sun blazed down on her. It might be December everywhere else, but in L.A. it felt like August.

She walked around her car. Sure enough, the right front tire was flat. She had a spare and a jack. She even knew how to change the tire. Assuming she could get the lug nuts unfastened.

She glanced at her watch, groaned at the time, then reached for her cell phone. No way she was going to be ready by five.

Seconds later the call was picked up. "Mr. Patrick's line."

"Annie McCoy for Duncan."

"Of course, Ms. McCoy. I'll put you right through."

"Another crisis?" Duncan asked when he took the call.

"Yes. I have a flat tire. I'll be a little late.

Do you want me to meet you there?"

"You need new tires."

She stared at the worn treads and rolled her eyes. "Obviously. I'll get them. I've been saving. In another two months I'll have enough."

"It's nearly the rainy season. You need them before then."

Probably, but no amount of needing brought in more money each month. She rubbed her temple, feeling the exhaustion creep into her bones. She'd been out late every night this week and still had to get up early for school. Fifteen five-year-olds kept her running all day. The last thing she needed was Duncan stating the obvious.

"I appreciate the heads-up," she said, trying not to sound as annoyed as she felt. "Look, it's hot, I'm tired. Just tell me what you want me to do."

"Let me buy you the tires."

"No." She drew in a breath. "No, thank you."

"You're supposed to be where I say, when I say. If new tires are required to get you there, then you'll get new tires."

"That is not a part of our deal," she told him, angry and sad at the same time. "You're not buying me tires. You're not buying me anything else. The freezer was too much, and I've already accepted that."

"Why are you mad?"

"I just am." She wanted to get out of the sun and heat. She wanted to curl up somewhere and sleep for two days. But mostly she didn't want to be Duncan Patrick's charity case.

"Annie? Talk to me."

"I don't have anything to say. I'll meet you there. I know how to change a tire. It won't take long."

He was silent. Worry replaced annoyance.

"Duncan, I'm sorry I snapped. I know this is part of our deal. I'm not backing out of it."

"Is that what you think? That after all this time, I would pull your brother out of rehab and toss him in jail?"

"No, but . . ."

"Which means yes."

"It means I owe you. I'm just crabby. It's hot, I'm tired. Let me get home and dressed and I'll be better."

"No," he said. "Just go home. You've got the Christmas play at school tomorrow night. You have to be rested for that."

"Winter festival," she corrected.

"Right. Because everyone is fooled."

"Exactly." Her bad mood faded a little. "I want to come to the party."

"No, you don't. Go home. Rest. It's okay."

She could take a bath, she thought wistfully. Sip some wine from the box. "Really?"

"Yes. About the tires . . ."

She groaned. "Don't make me have to hit you the next time I see you. I have a great jab."

"You have a sad excuse for a jab. It would be like being attacked by a butterfly."

Probably true, she thought. "You're not buying me tires."

"What if I set up an employee discount? I buy a lot of tires for my trucks. I have a service bay here. If it was available to everyone who worked here, would you use it?"

She would guess a lot of Patrick Industries employees would appreciate the discount as much as she would. For the greater good, she told herself. "After I see the announcement in writing."

"You're a tough negotiator."

"I spend my day dealing with five-year-olds. I have skills."

"I can see that. Are you okay changing the tire? I could send someone."

"By the time he got here, I'd be finished. I've done this before."

"Call me when you get home so I know you're okay."

The request stunned her. "Um, sure. I will."

"Okay. Bye."

"Bye."

She pressed the end button to disconnect the call, then walked around to the trunk where the jack and spare waited.

Suddenly it wasn't nearly as hot as it had been and she wasn't tired anymore. Duncan wanted her to let him know she was all right. He worried about her. Maybe it wasn't much, but as it was all she had, she was going to hang on to it with both hands.

Friday evening, Annie checked to make sure all her students were in their white men's T-shirts, with the fabric wings sewn on the back. Glitter-covered cardboard halos bounced over the five-year-olds' small heads. Once everyone was accounted for, she took a second to glance through the edge of the thick drapes to see if Duncan had arrived. Something she'd been doing every half minute or so since she'd arrived.

He still wasn't there. Which was fine, she told herself. He'd said he would *try* to get there, which was probably a polite way of saying he wasn't interested. It wasn't as if they were really dating. What gorgeous single guy wanted to spend Friday night with a bunch of other people's kids?

She held in a sigh as she backed away from the drapes. Only to bump into something warm and solid.

She turned and saw Duncan standing behind her.

"What are you doing here?" she blurted.

"You asked me to come."

She laughed, hoping she wasn't blushing. "No, I mean backstage."

"I wanted to say hi before the program started. One of the moms is saving me a seat."

Annie took in the broad shoulders, the strong features and the way he filled out his suit. "I'll just bet she is."

"What?"

"Nothing. Thanks for coming. You didn't have to."

"I wanted to see if you were still pissed."

"I was never pissed."

Humor brightened his gray eyes. "Now you're lying about it."

"I'm not. I was annoyed. There's a difference."

"You were pissed. You were practically screaming about the tires. Talk about shrill."

He was teasing, which she liked a lot. Back when they'd first met, she would never have imagined it possible.

"I was calm and rational," she told him.

"You were a girl. Admit it."

"I could hit you right now."

"You could and no one would notice. Especially not me." He took her arm and led her into a shadowy alcove. "Here." He handed her a piece of paper.

She looked at it. The sheet was a printout of a memo, detailing the new policy on discounted tires.

"Now will you get your damn car fixed?"

She stared at him, knowing that while he'd been helping her, he was also helping a lot of other people. "I will," she said, raising herself onto tiptoes and lightly kissing him. "I promise."

He put his arms around her and pulled her close. "Good. You're a pain in the ass. You know that, right?"

She giggled. "Yes. You're dictatorial. And annoying."

They hung on to each other for several seconds. Annie loved the feel of him, the strength and heat of his body. As always, being close to him made her feel safe.

"I have to get back to my class," she said reluctantly. "They're wearing cardboard halos that won't really survive very long."

"Okay. I'll see you after the Christmas thing."

"Winter festival."

"Whatever. I'll see you."

"Yes," she said and watched him walk away.

She knew then that despite the fact that she'd only known him a few weeks, she was well on her way to being in love with him. He was unlike anyone she'd ever met. He was better in every way possible.

He'd promised not to ask her to be friends and she trusted him to keep his word. But he'd also promised when the holiday season was over, so was their relationship. And she knew he would keep his word on that, as well. Wishing for more wouldn't change the outcome. Duncan had told her once that, in his life, somebody always won and somebody always lost. This time, she had a bad feeling the loser would be her.

Monday morning Duncan walked into his office to find a plate of cookies on his desk. They were covered in holiday plastic wrap and there was a handwritten note attached.

Dear Mr. Patrick,

Thank you so much for the new tire discount you announced on Friday. I'm a single mom with three kids and money is always tight. I've needed new tires for a while now and simply couldn't afford them. The discount means safer driving for my family.

I've always enjoyed working for Patrick Industries. Thank you for giving me another reason to be proud of my place of employment.

Have a wonderful holiday season.

Sincerely,
Natalie Jones
Accounts Payable

Duncan had no idea who the woman was or how long she'd worked for the company. He unwrapped the cookies and bit into one. Chocolate chip. His favorite.

Still chewing, he crossed to the windows overlooking the six-story atrium in the center of the building. He could see people coming in to start their week. People he'd never bothered to get to know.

Ten years ago, he would have been able to name every employee. He'd worked twenty-hour days, struggling to make the company profitable, then to grow it as quickly as possible. For the past few years, he'd had contact with his senior management team, his assistant and no one else. He didn't have time.

Who were these people who worked for him? Why had they chosen this company and not another? Did they like their jobs? Should that even matter to him?

He looked back at the note and the plate of cookies. Annie would be a disaster as a boss, giving away more than the company made. But maybe it was time for him to leave the confines of his office and remember what it was like to know his employees. To listen instead of command. To ask instead of demand. Maybe it was time to stop being the meanest CEO in the country.

# NINE

Duncan had never really enjoyed his board of director meetings, but this was worse than usual. Not because they were complaining — that he could handle. It was the way they were all *smiling* at him. Beaming, really, as if with pride. What the hell was up with that?

"The last two articles on you have been excellent," his uncle said. "Very positive."

"Just doing what we agreed."

"This reporter . . ." One of the board members adjusted his glasses and frowned at the business journal. "Charles Patterson seems to think you've had an awakening. Who's this Annie person?"

"Annie McCoy," Lawrence said, before Duncan could answer. "The woman Duncan's seeing."

The other board members looked at him.

"You told me to find someone nice," he reminded them. "She's a kindergarten teacher. Very pretty. Charles has a crush on her."

"Well done," the oldest board member said. "You should bring her around here so we can all meet her."

"There's no need for that," Duncan said, thinking the last thing Annie needed was a bunch of old guys trying to flirt with her.

"Annie's special," Lawrence announced. "Good for Duncan, too."

Duncan narrowed his gaze. "I'm seeing her through the holidays. It's a business arrangement, nothing more. You told me to find someone nice and clean up my act. I did. Don't make it more than it is."

"It didn't look like a business arrangement to me," Lawrence said.

"Looks can be deceiving."

There was no way he was telling his uncle or anyone on the board that he also thought Annie was special. They didn't need to know how she'd wormed her way into his life. The kicker was he didn't think she'd even been trying. But regardless of his feelings for her, when the holidays were over, so was their relationship.

The board moved on to other business. When they were finished, Lawrence lingered in the conference room until the other men had left.

"Are you serious about ending things with Annie?" his uncle asked. "I saw you two together, Duncan. You like her. You should marry her."

Duncan shook his head. "I've been married."

"To the wrong woman. I don't know what Valentina wanted, but it wasn't you or a real marriage. Annie's different. She's the kind of girl you spend forever with."

This from a man who'd been married five times? "You know this how?"

"I've lived a lot longer than you. I've seen things, made bad choices. There are few regrets more painful than knowing you let the woman of your dreams get away. You've always been smarter than me about most things. Don't be an idiot now."

"Thanks for the advice," Duncan said, standing up to leave.

"But you're not going to take it."

"I did what the board asked. That's all you're getting from me."

Lawrence stared at him for a long time. "Not everyone leaves."

Duncan didn't react to the statement, even though he knew the old man was wrong. Nearly everyone who mattered left. He'd learned that a long time ago. It was better not to care. Safer.

"Annie doesn't leave," his uncle added softly. "Look at her life."

"What do you know about it?"

"What you told me. She has her cousins and their friend living with her. She's helping to pay for their college educations. She agreed to date you to help her brother, after he tried to throw her under the bus. She's not a person who gives up easily."

True, Duncan thought uneasily. Annie took responsibility, hanging on with both hands. "That's different," he said.

"It's not and you know it. Annie scares the hell out of you because with her, everything is possible. Don't let what happened before ruin this for you. Don't live with regrets about letting her go. They'll eat you alive."

"I'll be fine."

"You can keep telling yourself that, but it won't be true. You've never been afraid of anything but risking your heart. Annie's the closest to a sure thing you're ever going to find."

Duncan found himself wanting to listen, which would only lead to trouble. "Annie got into this to save her brother. It has nothing to do with caring about me."

"Maybe it didn't, but it does now. Just pay attention. All the signs are there. She's falling for you. Maybe she's already in love with you. Chances like this don't come along very often. Trust me, you don't want to blow this one."

Lawrence walked out of the conference room. Duncan stood there, alone, wondering if the old man was telling the truth. Would he regret letting Annie go? In time he would find out. His uncle was also right about Annie scaring the crap out of him. There were possibilities with her. Great ones.

But he'd already given his heart to someone. He'd already believed in forever, and he'd learned a hard lesson. Love was an illusion, a word women used to sucker punch men. Maybe Annie was different, but he didn't know if he was willing to take the chance.

Despite three late nights at the office, getting by on minimal sleep and a workout schedule that would exhaust an elephant, Duncan still couldn't get his uncle's words out of his mind. He couldn't stop thinking about Annie.

Taking a chance violated everything he knew to be true and yet . . . he was tempted. It was the only possible explanation for his being in a mall less than a week before

Christmas, fighting the crowds and looking for presents for her cousins and Kami.

He should have had his assistant buy something online, he told himself, as yet another shopper stepped in front of him without looking. What did he know about the wants and needs of college-age girls? He was about to leave the department store when he saw a sign that proclaimed every woman loved cashmere.

There was a display of sweaters in an array of colors. A well-dressed salesperson came up and smiled. "Are you buying something for your wife or girlfriend?"

"Her cousins," he said. "And a friend. They're in college. Does cashmere work?"

"Always. You don't happen to know sizes, do you?"

He shrugged, then pointed to a young mother walking by. "About like that?"

"Got it. Do you want to pick the colors?"

"No."

"Should I gift wrap?"

"That would be great."

"Give me fifteen minutes and it will all be done. There's a coffee bar over by shoes, if you want to get away from the crowd."

He nodded and wandered in the direction of coffee, only to be stopped by a display of Christmas trees. They were small, maybe two feet, covered with twinkling white lights and miniature ornaments. The one that caught his eye was done in white and gold and decorated with dozens of angels.

They were all blonde and innocent, with big eyes. For some reason, they reminded him of Annie. He picked up the tree and carried it to the register.

Annie glanced anxiously at the box of fudge next to her. Despite her sudden stop at the unexpected light change, the box stayed firmly on the passenger seat of her car. Normally she was a careful driver who anticipated stops, but tonight she couldn't seem to get herself together. Probably because Duncan had completely rattled her with his invitation to "drop by."

They were in a lull — a four-day stretch with no parties — right before the last-minute craziness started. On Thursday, there was a party every night through Christmas Eve. When she'd first seen the party schedule, she'd been excited about the break, but now she found herself missing being around him. The four days, and nights, had seemed endless.

And then he'd called, inviting her over.

Why? She wanted it to be because he was missing her, too, but she couldn't be sure.

There was no reason to think anything about their relationship had changed — at least not from his end. She was in serious danger of falling desperately in love with him, which, if she'd thought things through at the beginning, shouldn't be a surprise. Handsome, smart, funny, caring man suddenly in her life. What was there not to like?

If only, she thought, before shaking her said. No. She was going to be sensible. Falling in love might be inevitable, but she wasn't going to let herself be swept away by her feelings. When this was over, pride might be the only thing she had left. She needed to remember that.

She parked in the guest spot, then took the elevator to his penthouse condo. Duncan opened the door right away.

"Thanks for coming," he said, his gray eyes dark with a smoldering need that made her thighs tremble.

"Thanks for asking me." She held out the box of fudge. "I made this. I don't know if you like chocolate. If not, you could take it into the office or . . ."

Instead of taking the candy, he grabbed her wrist and pulled her inside. The second the door closed behind her, she was in his arms, his mouth on hers.

She hung on as the world began to spin.

There was only the heat and the man and how she felt pressed up against his strength. He was already aroused, his hardness flexing against her belly. She managed to shove the fudge onto a table by the door and drop her purse, before hanging on to him with both hands.

She parted her lips and he deepened the kiss. Their tongues danced, touching, tracing, playing an erotic game. He bent her over slightly, then straightened, pulling her up off the floor.

Instinctively, she wrapped her legs around his hips. Despite being up in the air, she felt safe. Duncan would never drop her. He carried her into the bedroom, then slowly lowered her to the carpet. When her feet touched solid ground, he drew back, put his hands on her shoulders and turned her to face the room.

On the dresser there was a tiny Christmas tree. White lights twinkled, the only source of light in the huge room. She could see little angel ornaments on every branch.

Her throat got a little tight. "I thought you didn't want a tree," she whispered.

"I saw it and thought of you."

The words, whispered in her ear, made her eyes burn. Telling herself he wouldn't appreciate a girly show of emotion, she did her best to blink them away. He hugged her, pulling her close. She turned in his embrace and stared into his gray eyes.

Emotions raced through her. Not just desire, but love. There was no escaping the truth. She loved Duncan with all her heart. Whatever might happen, however it might end, she loved him.

The feeling was different, more powerful than anything she'd ever experienced. Getting over him would take a whole lot of time and effort, because as much as she wanted to believe everything would work out, she tried to be a realist. Her and Duncan? On what planet?

But for now there was the night and the man and she was determined to have as much as possible of both. She leaned into him, claiming him with a kiss. She couldn't tell him how she felt, but she could show him, she thought as she traced the powerful muscles in his arms.

She raised the hem of his sweater and ran her fingers across his broad chest. He took the hint and pulled off the sweater, then tossed it away. She pressed her lips to his breastbone, tasting his warm skin.

For a second, he was passive, accepting her caress. Then he reached for her, cupping her face and kissing her.

Even as they held on to each other, he was moving her toward the bed. When the backs of her legs bumped the mattress, he stopped. He pulled back enough to pull off her knit shirt. She stepped out of her shoes. Then they were tumbling onto the bed, him landing next to her.

They reached for each other. Even as they kissed, she reached for the hooks on her bra. She wanted to feel her bare breasts against his chest. He pushed her hands away and unfastened the bra in one easy movement. The lace-covered garment went flying.

Her jeans followed, as did his. She barely had time to notice that his briefs were also gone, before he settled his hand on her stomach.

Up or down, she thought, rolling onto her back. Either would work for her. He could move up or down. Another moment of hesitation and his fingers moved down. When he reached the barrier of her panties, he gripped the elastic and peeled them down. His large, strong hands made the return trip slowly, massaging as he went, teasing the insides of her knees before trailing up her thighs. He moved closer and closer to the promised land, but didn't touch her most sensitive spot. She held her breath, wanting, desperate, willing to do anything to have him touch her there. While he kissed her breasts, he rubbed his fingers against her inner thigh, then up onto her belly, making her squirm in anticipation.

Finally, slowly, he shifted again and slid through her swollen flesh. He touched the tiny center of her pleasure. A shiver raced through her. Gently at first, never pressing too hard or going too fast, he began to circle. Slowly, then a little more quickly, pushing her forward. She rotated her hips in time with him. Sensations raced through her. Muscles tensed. There was nothing but the movements and how he made her feel. Closer and closer still. Until the fall was inevitable.

She hung suspended for a brief moment. Intense pleasure pulsed through her and then she was falling. She came over and over, shuddering and moaning. He continued to touch her, gently, lightly, drawing out her release.

When she opened her eyes, he was watching her. His gray eyes seemed to see down to her soul. She smiled slowly, then kissed him.

"Thank you. That was . . . nice."

His eyebrows shot up. "Nice?"

She laughed. "Very nice. Extremely nice."

"You're crushing my ego."

She reached between them and stroked his erection. "Your ego seems to be doing just fine. We should take advantage of that."

"If you insist."

"I do."

In a matter of seconds, he put on a condom and was nudging at her thighs. She shifted to welcome him.

He filled her with one long, steady thrust. She felt herself stretching as he pushed in again and again. The sensation was delicious. Pleasure hardened his features, pulling at the muscles. His eyes were closed.

She closed hers as well, enjoying the ride — focusing on him and what he was feeling. She was so aware of his movements that at first she didn't even notice the pressure deep inside. The sort of tingling ache, the instinct to move against him, increasing the friction. The need started slowly, then grew more frantic. She found herself clinging to him, wanting him to go faster, deeper, harder.

She opened her eyes and found Duncan watching her. She couldn't control herself. This wasn't quiet, almost-boring sex. This was messy, frenzied desire. She held on to his upper arms, pumping her hips with each thrust. She opened her mouth to gasp in a breath and found herself panting. Her body wasn't her own. There was a driving force she didn't understand and couldn't control. There were —

Her climax caught her off guard. One second she was doing her best to catch her breath and the next she was lost in a shuddering, convulsing release that caused her to arch her back and cry out in a way she never had before. Her muscles tightened over and over again, then Duncan moaned and shuddered. They came together, a tangle of need and pleasure.

When they were done, Annie knew nothing would ever be the same again. She would never be the same. *She* might not be able to win Duncan, but she would never settle for anything less than loving someone with all her heart. That's what had been missing before, she thought, blissfully exhausted. True love and passion. An explosive combination.

Later, when Annie lay next to him, her head on his shoulder, his arm around her, she closed her eyes. She had to remember everything about this moment, everything that had happened. So later she could relive each moment in detail.

"Going to sleep?" he asked, his voice teasing.

"No. Enjoying the aftermath. Making love with you is pretty amazing."

"Thank you. Amazing is much better than nice."

She smiled, opened her eyes, then shifted so her chin was on his chest and she could stare into his eyes. "That's not what I mean. The other guys I was with — all two of them — weren't like you. Or maybe it was me. But I never felt . . ." She sighed. "It wasn't the same thrill ride."

He frowned. "Why not? Don't take this wrong, Annie, but you're easy."

She sat up, pulling the sheet with her so she stayed covered. Easy? She'd been thinking love and romance and he thought she was easy?

He sat up as well, then raised both hands. "I take it back. I should have said responsive. I've been with women who are difficult to get over the edge. You're not one of them." He smiled. "That's a good thing. Having you do what you do is the best kind of positive reinforcement."

"Oh. Okay."

"It wasn't like that with the other guys?"

"No. Sex was kind of . . . uninteresting." And she hadn't been truly in love with them. She got that now.

"No fireworks?"

"Not even a sputter. I liked it, but I never got the fuss." Now the fuss was perfectly clear. The fuss was her favorite part.

He shifted his pillow so it was behind his back, then leaned against the headboard. "Tell me about these guys."

"There's not much to say. I met Ron in college. He was studying engineering. I'm not sure he'd been with anyone before. I know I hadn't. We sort of figured it out together."

"Or not," Duncan said. "If you weren't happy."

"I was happy." She hadn't known there was more. Not physically or emotionally.

"Satisfied, then."

"I didn't know what to ask for. He was funny and smart and we had a good time. I thought everything was fine."

She and Ron had been together nearly three years. She thought she was in love with him and had assumed he felt the same way.

"At the beginning of our senior year, he ended things," she admitted. "He said he'd met someone else. That he didn't mean to hurt me, but she was the one. But that he and I should still be friends." She wrinkled her nose. "I passed on that offer."

"Smart move. And guy number two?"

Should there have been more men? Was two a small number? Duncan probably had dozens of women before and after Valentina.

"A.J.," she said with a sigh. "He was the assistant principal at my school. I met him my first day. We went out right away. Everything was so easy."

Duncan realized he'd made a huge mistake in asking about Annie's love life. While he wanted the information, he didn't like hearing about her with other men. The fact that the relationships had ended badly didn't change his sense of annoyance. He wanted to find both Ron and A.J. and beat the crap out of them. How dare either of them hurt Annie. Not that he wanted her with one of them now. He wanted her for himself.

Until the holidays were over, he reminded himself. Nothing more.

"He was also funny and smart. He loved kids." Annie shook her head. "I don't know. It was as if we were destined to be together. Everything fell into place. No complications. We were talking about getting married by our fifth date."

Something heavy seemed to fall into his stomach. He ignored the sensation. "What happened?"

"While I was dreaming about a June wedding, he got a job offer from a school in Baltimore. He wanted me to go with him. Jenny and Julie were seniors in high school and living with me. I couldn't just leave them. So he went without me. We agreed to date long distance, seeing each other once a month."

"Did you miss him?"

"Sure." She shifted so she was sitting next to him, then leaned her head against his shoulder. "I thought everything was fine. Over Memorial Day weekend, he told me while there wasn't anyone else, he wasn't interested in dating me anymore. Time away had shown him he wasn't as interested in me as he'd thought. But he would very much like us to be friends." She drew in a breath. "I never knew what went wrong."

He had a feeling she really meant to say what *she* had done wrong. But how to make her understand that none of this was about her? She'd found two stupid guys. It happened.

"Better to find out before you moved in with him rather than after."

She looked up at him, her blue eyes wide with shock. "I wouldn't live with him before we were married."

He held in a smile. "But you'd sleep with him."

"That's different. It's private. Living arrangements usually aren't. I'm a teacher. What would it say to my students if I lived with a guy without being married to him? What would it say to my cousins or Kami? Children don't learn by what we say, they learn by what we do."

Not ten minutes ago, she'd been screaming in his bed. Annie was nothing if not interesting. He could go his whole life and still not know everything about her.

"You're not giving up on Mr. Right, are you?" he asked.

"No. I'll find him." She leaned against his shoulder again. "I want to be married and have a family. I want to grow old with my husband, to be friends and lovers. I want to take care of him and have him take care of me. Which is all too traditional for you, huh?"

"I know how you enjoy your traditions."

"You don't believe in them."

"I got a tree. That's traditional."

"At least it's a start."

He sensed she needed more — needed him to make some kind of a promise. But he couldn't. He'd tried that once — trusting a woman with his heart.

Annie couldn't be more different than his ex. If he'd met Annie first . . . But he hadn't.

And being what she needed, what she deserved, was impossible. He hoped she understood that. Nothing about their deal had changed. When it was over, he would walk away — and he wouldn't offer to be just friends.

"Why are you walking like that?" Duncan asked. "Relax."

"I can't," Annie whispered, trying to look casual, but barely able to breathe.

It wasn't the fitted evening gown that was constricting her breathing, or the four-inch heels that altered her walk. Instead it was the weight of the necklace and earrings. Not their physical weight so much as their value.

She fingered the large diamond pendant hanging several inches below her throat. She didn't know much about fancy jewelry, but this was the biggest stone she'd ever seen. There were smaller diamonds leading to the platinum chain that held the piece securely around her throat. Matching earrings dangled in her upswept hair.

The jewelry ensemble had been delivered by a burly guard who had made Duncan sign several official-looking documents before he'd handed over the velvet cases containing the treasures.

"You're insured, right?" she asked quietly.

"If someone attacks me or a clasp breaks."

Duncan sighed. "I arranged for the jewelry because I thought you'd enjoy the pieces. I didn't mean for you to be nervous."

Probably true, she thought. A sweet gesture and one she really appreciated. Or she would, just as soon as she got over the burning need to vomit.

"Tell me they're not worth a million dollars and I'll relax."

He winked. "They're not worth a million dollars."

That was too easy. "You're lying."

"Me? How can you say that?"

Better not to know, she told herself as they walked into the elegant hotel ballroom. Fine. She would wear the borrowed jewelry and be excited that Duncan had wanted to make her happy. His actions were thoughtful and sweet. Once she got past the need to throw up, she would feel all quivery inside.

The party was large, with at least two hundred people milling about and talking. As a rule Annie didn't drink at any of the cocktail parties, but she might give in and have a glass of wine. With a crowd this big, no one would be having anything close to a serious conversation and she wouldn't be expected to do much more than smile and nod. Which meant her chances of messing up were that much less.

Besides, a little wine would make the idea of wearing all those diamonds more fun than terrifying.

As they moved through the crowd, Duncan kept her close. He held her hand in his, guiding them through the crush at the entrance. She saw an open area to her left.

"There's dancing," she said.

"I thought dancing with me made you nervous."

"Not anymore."

Their eyes locked. She didn't know what he was thinking, but she was remembering the last time they'd made love. When he'd made her feel things she hadn't known were possible and she accepted the fact that she was in love with him. No maybe, no almost. Just totally and completely in love with Duncan.

Fire flared in his gaze. She felt an answering heat in her belly.

"We don't have to stay long," he told her.

"Are you sure?" she asked, her voice teasing. "I was thinking we'd be here at least three or four hours."

He drew her close. "Fifteen minutes, tops. Or we could get a room in the hotel. The suites have jetted tubs."

"And you know this how?"

"Duncan?"

The person speaking his name had a low, sexy voice — the kind that belonged on radio. Annie turned and saw an incredibly tall, beautiful woman in a sexy black dress standing next to them. The woman smiled warmly, her blue eyes sparkling with delight.

"I was hoping to see you here," she said in her throaty voice. "I've missed you so much."

Duncan stiffened. Annie felt the tension fill his body as he turned toward the woman. "What the hell are you doing here?"

The smile never wavered. "I came to see you, Duncan." The woman glanced at Annie. "Are you going to introduce me to your friend?"

He hesitated, then released Annie's hand. "Annie, this is Valentina. My ex-wife."

# Ten

After convincing Annie to give him a few minutes, Duncan stood in the private alcove off the main ballroom, his arms folded across his chest, watching the woman he'd once wanted to spend the rest of his life with. Valentina stood completely still, gazing at him, a smile tugging at the corners of her lips.

"You look good," she said. "Time is such a bitch — always nicer to the men than the women."

"Why are you here?" he asked bluntly. "And spare me the bullshit."

The smile broadened. "There's no one quite like you, Duncan. My mistake was in thinking I could replace you."

"You mean do better? That was the point, wasn't it? Move up the food chain."

"Well, I suppose. I remarried, if that's what you're really asking. Eric was charming, easy to get along with." She wrinkled her nose. "Boring. I thought being rich was the most important thing in the world. I thought it gave me power and made me feel safe. I was wrong."

"Thanks for the update," he said. "I need to get back to the party."

"Wait, Duncan. Aren't you even a little happy to see me?"

He stared into her catlike eyes, then dropped his gaze to the full mouth that had known how to take him from zero to sixty in less than a minute.

When she'd first left, he'd been devastated. He'd retreated into anger, had vowed revenge, had understood the primal fury of a man longing to lock up the woman he loved. To keep her from the world. When the anger had ceased to burn quite as brightly, humiliation had joined rage. The knowledge that she had betrayed him, that he had been a fool, had kept him up nights.

He'd loved her. She had promised him everything he'd ever wanted and he'd believed her. That she would love him forever, that they would always be together. That he was the one.

Over time he'd accepted that he had been a means to an end. He'd looked back on their relationship and had seen her for what she was. The anger had faded, the wounds healed. A few days after she'd left, his uncle had told him that the opposite of love wasn't hate — it was indifference. Now, staring at the woman he'd once married, he knew that to be true.

"You don't matter enough for me to have any emotion on the subject," he said.

"Wow. Talk about honest. So you didn't miss me at all?"

He thought about those long nights when he'd lain awake, staring at the ceiling. He would have sold his soul for her return. Good thing the devil had been busy making deals with other people at the time.

"I loved you," he told her. "Having you leave hurt like a son of a bitch. So what? That was three years ago, Valentina. I've moved on."

"I wish I could say the same, but I haven't. I know I was wrong and I know I'll have to earn back your trust. That's why I'm here. I still love you, Duncan. I never stopped. I want us to have a second chance."

He heard the words, let them sink into his skin, then waited. Was there any part of him interested? Did a fiber or a cell long to be with her again? Were old scars still tender?

No, he thought with relief. There was nothing. Not a hint of longing or curiosity. She was nothing more than someone he used to know.

He started for the door. “Sorry. Not interested.”

Annie sat next to Duncan in his car. After he’d gone off with Valentina, she’d circled the ballroom, smiling at anyone who had made contact with her. He’d returned to her side about ten minutes later and had said they should leave.

So much for the romantic night in the hotel room, she thought sadly.

Duncan hadn’t spoken while they’d waited for the valet to bring around his car. Now, aware that he was driving to her place rather than his, she resigned herself to a very brief ending to their evening. If the girls weren’t home, they would be shortly. Inviting him in wouldn’t give them any time alone. She carefully removed the earrings, then the necklace and passed both back to him.

“Thank you for letting me wear these tonight.”

He took them and dropped them into his suit-jacket pocket. “You’re welcome. I’m sorry we didn’t stay longer. After Valentina showed up . . .” He tightened his grip on the steering wheel. “She’s back to make trouble.”

What she really wanted to ask was “What

did she say?" but lacked the courage, so instead she said, "How do you know?"

"She's breathing. I didn't know what kind of a scene she would make. Leaving seemed easier. I don't want you in the middle of anything."

"I appreciate that." She cleared her throat. "It must have been a shock, seeing her after all this time. It's been what? Three years?"

He nodded. "I could have gone a lot longer without having to deal with her again."

"You're going to be dealing with her?"

"I hope not, but my luck isn't that good. She wants something and she won't stop until she's made every attempt to get it."

Wanted something? As in money . . . or did Valentina want Duncan back? Annie told herself she should be happy if that was what was going on. A marriage repaired was a good thing. Assuming Valentina was sincere.

Annie told herself she was mature enough, in love enough, to want what was best for Duncan. The ache in her chest and the need to cry were beside the fact.

Duncan pulled up in front of her small house. "The party tomorrow will be easier. It's smaller. Quieter. I'll pick you up at six-thirty."

He barely glanced at her as he spoke, making her realize he wasn't even going to kiss her good-night. Holding in the hurt, she forced herself to smile as she got out of the car.

"Good night, Duncan. I'll see you tomorrow."

"Good night."

She barely had time to close the passenger door before he gunned the engine and drove off. She stood on the sidewalk, watching his taillights disappear.

Telling herself he hadn't broken the rules didn't make breathing any less painful. And wondering if he was returning to the party to be with Valentina only made her wish she could go back in time a couple of hours and keep the other woman from ever speaking to Duncan in the first place. Not that she could change the past the two of them shared. A past that was very likely going to have a big impact on her present.

"Okay, so owning a bank is even better than I thought," Annie said the following night as Duncan pulled up behind a Rolls, in front of a large Beverly Hills estate. "Didn't bankers take a financial hit in the past year or so?"

"Not all of them."

It had been nearly twenty-four hours since Duncan had dropped her off the previous evening. She'd spent about twenty of them trying to convince herself that even if she wasn't fine, she could pretend. Acting might not be her gift, but she would work at faking it. He'd been his normal self when he'd arrived to pick her up, so maybe last night was like a bad dream — something that would fade in the light of day.

When she climbed out of the car, she stared at the glittering three-story mansion. It was huge, with lights everywhere, a long, wide walkway and a fountain roughly the size of a semi.

"This rich thing," she said as Duncan moved next to her. "Looks like fun."

"The taxes would kill you," he said with a grin, then leaned in and kissed her on the mouth.

"Just paying for the lightbulbs would make me whimper." She leaned into him and laughed. "Do you think they take in boarders? I mean, a room in this place would be bigger than my whole house."

"Want me to get an application?"

"If they have them lying around."

He put his arm around her and they walked toward the front door. A uniformed butler let them in. They were shown to a massive living room with a roaring fire. Sofas and comfy-looking chairs filled the football field–sized space. To the left was a bar. In front of them were four sets of French doors leading out to a huge patio.

"There is a light buffet outside," the butler told them. "The area is heated and very comfortable."

Duncan thanked the man. Annie waited until he left before whispering, "So they're the reason L.A. is always warm in the winter. They're heating the whole outdoors. Interesting."

Duncan laughed and pulled her close. She wrapped her arms around him, feeling the vibration of the sound. Then it stopped and he tensed. She felt every muscle, heard the sudden increase in his breathing and knew, without turning around, that someone else had walked into the party.

"Duncan," she breathed.

He touched her cheek and stared into her eyes. "It doesn't matter."

But she had a feeling that it mattered a lot. More than either of them wanted to admit.

Annie stepped back and turned around. Valentina stood in the entrance to the beautiful home. Her eyes locked with Duncan's, but she didn't do anything more than nod at him before walking into the party.

"You going to be all right?" he asked, pressing his hand to the small of her back and guiding her outside.

"I'm fine," she lied.

What else was there to say? That Valentina terrified her? That she believed Duncan was still in love with his ex-wife? That she'd always known she didn't have a chance with Tim's boss, but she'd allowed herself to hope and it was all going to end badly? All she could do was pray that he remembered not to tell her he wanted to be friends. It was what she'd asked for, and Duncan was the type of man to remember.

Maybe the problem wasn't Valentina, she thought as they stepped outside. Maybe it was her. Maybe she should learn to ask for more.

Time crawled by. Annie did her best not to glance at her watch every five minutes. The party was small enough that she and Duncan had to stay for at least a couple of hours. So far they'd been outside and Valentina had stayed inside, avoiding each other. She wondered if that would last for the entire party.

When Duncan got into a conversation about oil futures, she excused herself and went in search of the restroom. It was as lovely as the rest of the house, complete with a marble vanity and dozens of expensive soaps, hand creams and hair products. After she'd washed her hands and fluffed her curls, she opened the door and stepped into the hallway. Only to find Valentina waiting for her.

Duncan's ex was dressed in black pants and a cream-colored off-the-shoulder sweater. She was tall, thin and beautiful, with the kind of sleek, straight hair Annie had always envied.

"Hi," Valentina said, clutching a martini glass. "You're Duncan's girlfriend, right?"

Annie nodded slowly. The truth was different, but Valentina didn't need to know about their deal.

"Have you been going out long?" the other woman asked.

"We met in September," Annie said, hoping she didn't look as nervous as she felt. "I, ah, had a flat tire and Duncan stopped to help."

"That doesn't sound like him at all. You're a teacher?"

"Kindergarten."

"Let me guess. You're sweet and kind. You take in orphans and stray pets."

Annie couldn't read the other woman's

voice. There was tension in it, but the source wasn't clear. Was she mocking Annie or herself?

"If you'll excuse me," Annie said, moving around her.

"Wait. Please. I . . ." Valentina set her drink on a small table and sucked in a breath. "I don't know how things are between you and it's really none of my business. I gave up any rights to Duncan a long time ago. I was stupid. I thought I could do better. I was wrong. It's not just that he's the best man I know, it's that I never stopped loving him."

Tears filled Valentina's blue eyes. One trickled down her cheek. She brushed it away impatiently.

"I want a second chance. I know it's practically impossible. He's not going to forgive me easily, but I have to try. Have you ever been in love? Have you ever known down to your bones that you'd finally found the only man on the planet who would complete you?"

Annie nodded slowly. She wanted to point out that love wasn't about being completed. It was about giving, not getting, but that wasn't the point.

"I love him," Valentina said. "Before, when we were together, he held so much of himself apart. I think it had something to do with his past. I was young and impatient. Now I know better. He's worth waiting for, fighting for. I made a mistake and he paid the price. I'm back for a second chance. I'm back to convince him how much he means to me. To me, he's my husband. He'll always be my husband. I want a chance to make our marriage work. Can you understand that?"

Annie nodded because it would hurt too much to speak. Valentina had said the only words that would have convinced her to give up. She couldn't argue against a chance of Valentina and Duncan making their marriage work. If they were successful, maybe he could let go of his fear of being left. Maybe he would learn to love again. Better Valentina than no one, she told herself. In time, she would even believe that.

The mall might be closed at three in the morning, but the Internet was always open. Annie clicked on a link, then stared at the picture of the painting. It was small, maybe twelve-by-twelve, with a plain black frame. The artist, a famous sports painter, had chosen boxing as his subject.

The colors were vivid, the expressions fierce. There was something about the way the two men stared at each other that reminded her of Duncan.

"Annie, what are you doing up?"

She smiled at Kami, who looked sleepy as she stepped into Annie's room.

"It's late," Annie said. "You have classes."

"I could see your light was still on."

"Oh. Is it bothering you?"

Kami sat on the edge of the bed and shook her head. "No. I'm worried about you. You were acting weird when you got home. Are you sick? Is this about Duncan? Did he hurt you?"

"Duncan's getting back together with his ex-wife."

"Since when?"

"It hasn't actually happened yet, but it probably will. I can't stand in the way of that. Not that I would be. I mean, he's just dating me because of our deal."

Kami wore her long dark hair in a thick braid. Her oversize T-shirt and PJ bottoms made her look young, but her eyes were wise. "He's not going out with you because he has to. Not anymore. He got his good press a while ago. Besides, what about the freezer and the food and the presents under the tree?"

A few days ago, a box of presents had been delivered. Well, presents for the girls. There hadn't been anything for her. At the time she'd told herself that he would give her something later. Privately. Now she wasn't so sure.

"She's still in love with him."

"So? She left him. The bitch had her chance. Now it's yours."

"While I appreciate the support, she's really not a bitch. I wish she was. Then I could hate her." And fight for Duncan. "They deserve a second chance."

"What about you? You're in love with Duncan."

"I'll get over it." She clicked on the Buy It Now button and tried not to wince at the price. She wanted to give Duncan something special. Something that would make him happy.

"You should tell him you love him," Kami said. "He needs to make an informed decision."

Annie managed a smile. "He's not buying auto insurance. He doesn't need to comparison shop."

"Maybe he needs to be reminded about what's important. You're the best thing that ever happened to him. If he doesn't see that, he's an idiot."

"Should I tell him that, too?"

"Absolutely."

■ ■ ■ ■

Annie arrived at Duncan's office shortly after four. She'd called and made an appointment, wanting to be sure she saw him. They were supposed to go out that night. Nearly their last event. A cocktail party. But he wouldn't need her for that or the other parties to follow. His reputation had been saved and he had more important things to do. Like get on with his life.

She'd spent the day telling herself that she had to do the right thing. That loving Duncan meant wanting what was best for him rather than for herself. That she had to be strong. Losing Ron and A.J. hadn't mattered. She'd recovered in a matter of weeks. But losing Duncan was different. She had fallen madly, hopelessly, totally in love with him.

She'd learned early that life could be a challenge. She'd been ten when her mom had first gotten sick and barely eighteen when she'd died. Her aunt wrestled with immobilizing depression, spending more time in hospitals than out. Over the years, Annie had helped raise her brother and her cousins. She'd always done her best. They were family and that mattered more than anything.

She'd made sacrifices, but nothing she regretted. It was her nature to give — she knew that. So the fact that she'd given her heart to Duncan shouldn't be a surprise. Nor was the reality that he didn't want it.

She waited outside his office door until four and then was shown in. Duncan put down his phone and smiled when he saw her.

"Why do we have an appointment?" he asked, walking around the desk to greet her. "I'm picking you up in a couple of hours."

He looked good, she thought, taking in the shape of his mouth, the breadth of his shoulders. His eyes — how could she ever have thought them cold? — brightened with pleasure. He smiled, then kissed her.

"Let me guess," he said. "You're here to convince me to start a profit-sharing plan."

"You can profit share with your employees? You should think about it."

Typical Annie, Duncan thought, leading her over to a sofa and sitting next to her. Good thing she'd never gone into business. She would have given away her entire worth the first day.

She'd come straight from school. He could tell by her clothes — the long plaid skirt, the cardigan covered with beaded snowmen. Her curls were mussed, her light makeup mostly faded. This wasn't the glamorous Annie he usually saw on their evenings together. This was more real, more beautiful.

She leaned toward him and covered his hands with hers. Her gaze was intense.

"Duncan, I talked to Valentina at the party last night."

His good mood vanished. Why wasn't he surprised? "Whatever she said, she's lying. You can't trust her, Annie. She'll do anything, say anything, to get what she wants."

"She wants you."

Annie paused, as if waiting for a reaction. His was to swear loudly, then punch the wall. Dammit all to hell. "You believed her."

"She loves you, Duncan. She realizes she made a mistake and wants to be with you again. You were married — you owe her the chance to try to make it work."

She believed her words. He could see the truth in her big blue eyes. There was something else there, too. Pain, maybe. Regret.

Or was he reading too much into the situation? What he knew about women couldn't fill a thirty-second commercial. He knew they lied and manipulated. That they only thought about themselves. That given the chance, they would sell out anyone to get ahead.

Well, not Annie. She seemed to be genuine. He'd seen her with her students, with her cousins, hell, even with his uncle. She was exactly what she appeared to be. Open, honest, smart and funny. She led with her heart, which made her a fool, but everyone had flaws.

"You're here to plead Valentina's case?" he asked. "Did she offer to pay you?"

"No. It wasn't like that. She cried. She's desperately in love with you. I didn't want to believe her at first, but then she asked me if I'd ever been in love. If I'd ever known down to my bones that someone was the one. She meant it. Every word."

He was a whole lot less convinced. "She's a good actress, Annie. Don't let yourself get too caught up in her pain. It's mostly for show."

"It's not. She's your wife."

"Ex-wife. It's been three years."

"Can you honestly say you're not in love with her? That she doesn't matter, that she never mattered?"

"Of course I thought I loved her when we got married," he said, frustrated. "I was a fool."

"You owe it to her and to yourself to hear her out."

He stood up and crossed to the window overlooking the atrium below. Folding his arms across his chest, he faced Annie.

"She got to you."

Annie stood. Tears filled her eyes, but she blinked them away.

"She begged me to get out of the way and that's what I have to do. I'm not going with you tonight, Duncan. Take Valentina instead. Give her a chance."

"We have a deal."

"It's nearly over anyway. What does it matter if we stop things now?"

He'd known his relationship with Annie was finite. He'd designed it that way himself. But until now, he hadn't been willing to look past the holidays, to the days after. When she would no longer be with him.

She was leaving. Just like they all left. Her excuse was noble, but the outcome was the same. She would be gone and he would be left here, without her.

They all left. No one could be trusted. No *woman* could be trusted. Anger burned hot and bright, but he knew it was merely a shield to something else that would taunt him for a very long time.

"Our contract is clear," he told her coldly. "You walk out now and I throw your brother in jail."

He braced himself for the anger, the tears, the threats. Instead she smiled.

"Oh, please, Duncan. We both know you won't. You're not that guy." The smile quivered a little, then died. "Do you think this is easy for me? It isn't. I love you. But look at you and your life. I don't belong there. I've had a wonderful time and you're a great man. You deserve every happiness. That's why it's important for you to give Valentina a second chance. You loved her once. Maybe it was just the wrong time for the two of you."

Once again she was speaking the truth as she knew it. Duncan thought he understood Annie, but he'd been wrong. She loved him and she wanted him to be with someone else? The ridiculousness of it made him even more angry.

"If you loved me, you'd stay," he said, his voice practically a growl. "Next you'll tell me you want to be friends."

She winced, as if he'd slapped her. "You're upset."

"You're playing a game. I expected better. If you want to leave, then go. Don't give me any bullshit about it being for my own good. That's crap and you know it."

Now the tears fell, but unlike those in other women, these tears seemed to burn him. He felt the searing all the way down to his heart.

"You're everything I ever dreamed about. You're strong and gentle. You're giving and funny. I want to spend my whole life with you. I want to sleep in your arms and have your children and love you and worry about you. I want to spend fifty years with you and have the neighbors say things like, 'Those Patricks have been married forever.' "

She wiped her face with her fingers. "But it's not just about me. There's Valentina. So I'm doing the right thing. Because that's important. But all it would take is one word, Duncan. I'm not fighting this because I didn't think there was a point. I didn't think you loved me back. Tell me it's totally over with her and that you love me. That you want me to stay, and I will."

He finally knew her end game. To trap him. "I'd be a great meal ticket," he said. "And I'll give you points for originality. That was quite a speech."

She stiffened as the color faded from her face. She wiped at her tears again, then picked up her purse.

"There's no winning, is there?" she asked quietly. "You told me and told me and I didn't listen. Maybe you're right about

Valentina and maybe I am. I hope you take the time to find out. As for me, if you can say those words, if you can really think I'm here because you're wealthy and successful, then you never knew me at all. And I guess I never knew you. Because the man I love can see into my heart and my soul. He knows who I am. And that's not you. Good-bye, Duncan."

And then she was gone.

# Eleven

Duncan hadn't been mind-numbingly drunk in years. Probably not since college, when he'd been young and stupid. Now he was older, but apparently just as stupid. He'd avoided work, blown off the last of the holiday parties and had holed up in his condo for three days. Now, hungover, dehydrated and feeling like something that had been dead for a month, he forced himself to shower and get dressed before stumbling into the kitchen and making coffee.

He'd lost before. His first three fights had been a disaster. He'd barely gotten in a single punch. His coach had told him to go find another sport. Maybe baseball, where the only thing that could hit him was the ball. But he hadn't given up and by his senior year of high school, half a dozen colleges were offering him a free ride.

Taking over the family business hadn't

been easy, either. He'd screwed up dozens of times, losing opportunities because of his youth and inexperience. But he'd persevered and now he had it all. But nothing in his life had prepared him for losing Annie.

Her words haunted him. "The man I love can see into my heart and my soul. He knows who I am. And that's not you." He would have preferred her to take out a gun and shoot him. The recovery would have been easier. Or at least faster.

He told himself that the bottom line was she'd left. She'd walked out. Telling him she loved him first only added a level of drama. He should respect that. And he could. The problem was he couldn't believe it. Annie didn't play games.

His doorbell rang. His head screamed at the sound. He made his way to the door and pulled it open. Valentina stood there, holding a package.

"This came for you," she said, handing over the flat box. "I told your doorman I'd bring it up myself."

She stepped into the condo and looked around. "It looks great, Duncan. I wish you'd kept our old place, though. There was so much room. Still, we can buy something else. Maybe a house, this time." She moved toward him and lightly kissed him. "How are you? Your assistant said you hadn't been feeling well. You're really pale."

He recognized Annie's neat writing on the package. As much as he wanted to open it, he wouldn't until he was alone. He set it on the dining room table, then returned to the kitchen. The coffee was ready.

He poured a cup and took a long drink. When he felt the heated liquid hit his belly, he turned back to face his ex-wife.

Valentina had dressed in winter-white. From her suede boots to her fuzzy sweater, she was a vision of sexual elegance. The woman knew how to wear clothes, he thought. And take them off for anyone interested.

"Why are you here?" he asked, taking another swallow.

"I want to talk to you, Duncan. About us. I meant what I said. I still love you. I want a second chance."

He looked her up and down. She was still preternaturally an ice queen if there ever was one. At one time she'd been all he'd wanted.

"And if I said I needed to test-drive the merchandise before I made a decision?" he asked.

She smiled. "Anytime."

"Kids?" She'd never wanted children. Too

messy and she ran the risk of screwing up her figure.

"Of course." She tilted her head. "And a dog. Please. You can't have children without having pets. They need to learn about responsibility."

"The kids or the dog?" He reached for his coffee. "Never mind. You're serious about this?"

"Yes, Duncan. I still love you and am willing to do anything to prove that."

Uh-huh. "Including signing a prenup? One that gives you absolutely no part of my business or personal fortune. Now or in the future? You wouldn't get a penny, Valentina. Ever."

He would guess that Botox shots kept her from frowning, but there was no mistaking the tightening of her mouth or the stiffening of her body.

"Duncan," she began, then sighed. "Shit."

He wasn't even surprised. "So it is about the money."

"In part," she admitted. "And proving a point. Eric left me. *Me.* I was going to end things, but he beat me to it, the bastard. I wanted to prove a point. Show him what he'd lost."

Pride, he thought. He could respect that. "Sorry I can't help," he said.

"Are you pissed?"

"More relieved."

"Excuse me?" she said, walking to the coffee and pouring herself a mug. "You would be nowhere without me. I took a rough, ill-mannered street kid and turned him into a gentleman."

"You screwed my business partner, on my desk."

"I know. I'm sorry about that."

"It doesn't matter anymore."

"But it was still tacky. I am sorry." She looked at him. "You look good. I mean that. You've come a long way."

They talked for a few more minutes, then Valentina left. Duncan closed the door behind her, relieved to have her out of his life. This time for good. Then he crossed to the table and opened the package from Annie.

Inside was a painting of two boxers. He knew the artist, had a larger piece of his work in his study.

There was a note inside. No, a Christmas card.

*This made me think of you.*

Duncan studied the masterful work and could guess the approximate price she'd paid. It was a whole lot more than she could afford. Why would she have done this? He checked the date. She'd had it shipped *after* she'd ended things. Who did that? What was she playing at?

He didn't have any answers, a circumstance he didn't like. He wanted his life simple — predictable. But Annie was anything but. She demanded too much. She wanted him to do the right thing, to be a better man. She wanted him to love her back.

Back. Meaning he believed she loved him in the first place? And if he did, what was he doing, letting her get away?

"Very upscale," Annie said, hoping it sounded more like a tease than nervousness. She sat across from Tim in a comfortable wicker chair on a patio behind the rehabilitation housing where her brother was staying.

"It's nice," he said.

He sat across from her, relaxed and tanned, more calm than she'd seen him in years. This was the first Saturday visitors had been allowed. Annie had arrived right at ten and Tim had been waiting for her. So far their conversation had consisted of greetings and the weather.

She picked at the wicker on the arm of the chair, then glanced across the broad lawn. Judging from the uneasy body language she saw in the other visitors, she wasn't the only one who didn't know what to say.

"Are you . . ." she began.

Tim leaned toward her and smiled. "It's okay. You did the right thing. I didn't believe that until a few days ago, but now I know you were right. I needed help. I still need help."

Relief rushed through her. She grabbed his hand and squeezed. "Yeah?"

He nodded. "I was chasing the dream, Annie. So sure that if I kept trying, I'd hit it big. It's what you always say about kids who cheat in school. If they would put half the effort into studying, they'd get a good grade. But instead they want to play the system. I want to play the odds. The trouble is, the odds are never in my favor."

"Which means what?" she asked.

"I have a gambling problem. I need to stay away from it. No blackjack, no Vegas, not even a raffle ticket. It's going to take a while, but I'll beat this, Annie."

She stared into her brother's blue eyes and felt relief. "I'm glad," she whispered.

"Me, too." He pulled free and shifted on his seat. "About what I said. I'm sorry."

"I know."

"I can't believe I stole that money. What an idiot. I really appreciate the deal you made with my boss. Anyone else would have let me go to jail."

"I couldn't do that."

"It's what I deserved."

"But not what you needed."

"I know. I've been in touch with Mr. Patrick. He says I can have my job back." Tim smiled self-consciously. "Sort of. I won't have access to any of the bank accounts. I'll have to earn his trust again, but I will. We worked out a payment plan for me to reimburse him."

Tim had talked to Duncan? Annie wanted to ask how he was. She missed him more than she had ever imagined, and she'd known it would be bad.

"I'm glad," she said.

"I want to pay you back, too," Tim told her.

"You don't owe me anything."

"Sure I do. Look what you did for me, Annie."

"I went to a bunch of parties. It wasn't work."

She'd also fallen in love and gotten her heart broken, but that wasn't anything Tim needed to hear right now. She would tell him later, when he was stronger.

"I'll make it up to you," Tim promised.

"All I need is for you to get your life back together," she said. "Be happy. That's enough."

Her brother stood and pulled her to her feet, then hugged her.

"You're the best," he said. "Thank you."

She hung on, willing him to heal. Because if he was all right, then this had been worth it. As for herself, and the aching emptiness inside, there was nothing to be done except hope that eventually she, too, would find her way back.

Duncan walked into the crowded Westwood restaurant. The hostess smiled at him. "Sir, do you have a reservation?"

"No."

"I'm sorry, we're booked. It's Christmas Eve and we're only having service until seven."

"I'm not here for dinner," he told her, looking into the dining room. "I want to see one of your servers. Jenny." He spotted her. "Never mind. There she is."

"Sir, you can't disturb our guests."

Duncan forced himself to flash her a smile. "Don't worry. I won't."

He wove through tables until he was next to Jenny. "We have to talk," he told her.

She barely glanced at him. "No, we don't."

She headed for the kitchen. He followed, grabbing her arm before she could disappear behind the swinging doors.

The restaurant hummed with conversation. Christmas carols played over the speakers. In the kitchen came the call for more turkey, as waiters and cooks battled for space.

Jenny glared at him, her blue eyes so much like Annie's. They were about the same height, too.

"I've been looking for her," he said. "I've been everywhere I can think of. Jenny, you have to help me."

The college student glared at him. "No way. You're nothing but a soul-sucking bastard. Do you know she cries every night? She doesn't want us to know, so she waits until she goes to bed. But we can hear her. She loved you and you hurt her."

"I know. I let her go and I'll regret that until the day I die. I was wrong. She's amazing and beautiful and so much more than I deserve. I love her, Jenny. I swear, I just want to take care of her. So please, tell me where she is."

Jenny hesitated, as if trying to decide.

"It's Christmas," he said. "A time for miracles. Can't you believe that I've changed?"

"I don't know," she admitted.

He stared into Jenny's eyes. "I love that she would sell her soul to save her brother. And when she's really stressed, she goes for M&M's. I love that she's never quite mastered the art of walking in high heels, so sometimes she has to grab the wall to keep from stumbling. I love how she sees the best in everyone, even me, and believes that everything is possible."

He cleared his throat. "I love how she let you and Julie and Kami live with her and that she would accept a new freezer because it would feed the three of you, but fought me on new tires that would keep just her safe. I love how she smiles at her students, how she worries about being a role model. I love how she takes care of the world. But who takes care of her? Who watches out for her and looks after her? Who takes over so she can rest? I want to be that guy, Jenny. I want to be the one."

He stopped talking, only to realize the restaurant had gone quiet. He glanced around and saw everyone was staring, listening. A couple of the men looked embarrassed, but the women were all smiling and nodding.

Jenny drew in a breath. "I swear, if you

hurt her again . . ."

"I won't." He pulled the jewelry box out of his jacket pocket. "I want to marry her."

"Okay," she breathed. "She's at church. They called earlier and needed someone to help with the decorations. Apparently everyone has the flu and there's a midnight service." Jenny gave him the address. "Don't screw this up," she warned.

He kissed her cheek. "I won't. I promise."

Annie carried pots of poinsettias until her arms ached. When they were all in place, she adjusted the white lights, then plugged them in. The soft glow made the leaves seem to glisten. She'd already distributed the special booklets of Christmas carols, and attached beautiful sprays of roses and pine to the end of each pew. The candles were in place.

"You've done enough for twenty," Mary Alice, the minister's wife, told her. "Get along home, Annie. You need to rest a little or you'll be nodding off during the midnight service."

"All right. If you're sure."

"Thank you for answering my call for help. I hated to bother you, but I knew my old bones would keep me from getting everything done on time and Alistair is visiting with a member who's in the hospital. Everyone else . . ." Mary Alice smiled. "You were a blessing. Thank you."

"You're more than welcome. See you soon."

Annie turned to leave, telling herself she liked being able to help. And as everyone else had been busy in her family, it was a good thing she'd been home to receive the call. It was nearly Christmas. She refused to be sad. Or feel alone. She was lucky. Her brother was healing, her cousins were doing well. She had a great job and friends and so much to be thankful for. If there was an empty place inside, well, it would heal. By this time next year she would be her old self again.

She walked out a side door to the parking lot. It was already dark but still warm. This was going to be another Christmas with seventy-degree weather. One day she would spend the holidays where it was cold. A white Christmas. But for now, she would enjoy the fact that she didn't even need a coat.

She headed for her car, but before she got there, someone moved out of the shadows. A man. Duncan.

She came to a stop. Her heart pounded hard and fast, her chest got tight. She wanted to cry and laugh and throw her arms around him. She'd missed him so much.

"Annie," he said, then smiled at her.

And she knew. It was there in his warm gray eyes. The truth, the love. How he'd realized what was important, how he knew she was the one. Warmth and happiness flooded her. She felt as if she could float or even fly.

Without thinking, she threw herself at him. He caught her and pulled her against him, holding on as if he would never let go.

Home, she thought. She was finally home.

"Annie," he said again. "I love you."

"I know."

He laughed. "You can't know. I have a whole speech prepared. I have to tell you what I've learned and how I've changed and why you can trust me."

He slowly lowered her to the ground. Her feet hit the pavement, but she didn't let go. Instead she stared into his face, feeling the love spilling out of him.

"I already know all that."

He touched her cheek. "Valentina was in it for the money. Not that it matters. I was never interested in being with anyone but you."

"I want to say I'm sorry it didn't work out, but I'm really not." She laughed. "I guess that's bad, huh?"

"No. I feel the same way. Do you want to hear the speech?"

"Maybe later." Right now she just wanted to be with him, to feel him close and know that he loved her. This was perfect. She'd been given Duncan for Christmas.

"At least let me do this part." He pulled a small box out of his jacket pocket, then right there in the church parking lot, dropped to one knee.

"I love you, Annie McCoy," he said. "I will always love you. Please say you'll marry me. I'll spend the rest of my life making your dreams come true."

He opened the box and she gasped when she saw the huge diamond nestled there.

"Duncan? Really? You want to marry me?"

"Don't doubt me, Annie. You're the one. Now that I've found you, I'll never let you go."

She didn't know how or why she'd gotten so lucky, but she was grateful. She bent down and kissed him.

"Yes, I'll marry you."

He laughed, then stood and slid the ring on her finger. Then they hung on to each other as if they would never let go.

"I've missed you," he whispered. "I've been lost without you."

"Me, too."

"You've changed me. How did I get so lucky?"

"That's what I was thinking. That I got so lucky to find you," she admitted, then opened her eyes. A brilliant star winked in the sky. She pointed. "Look."

He turned. "It's just Venus."

"Don't tell me that. Can't it be a Christmas miracle?"

"If it makes you happy."

"It does."

"Then that's what it is." He kissed her. "Merry Christmas, Annie."

"Merry Christmas, Duncan."

# ABOUT THE AUTHOR

**Susan Mallery** is a *New York Times* best-selling author of more than ninety romances. Her combination of humor, emotion and just-plain-sexy has made her a reader favorite. Susan makes her home in the Pacific Northwest with her handsome husband and possibly the world's cutest dog. Visit her Web site at www.SusanMallery.com.

We hope you have enjoyed this Large Print book. Other Thorndike, Wheeler, Kennebec, and Chivers Press Large Print books are available at your library or directly from the publishers.

For information about current and upcoming titles, please call or write, without obligation, to:

Publisher
Thorndike Press
295 Kennedy Memorial Drive
Waterville, ME 04901
Tel. (800) 223-1244

or visit our Web site at:

http://gale.cengage.com/thorndike

OR

Chivers Large Print
published by AudioGO Ltd
St James House, The Square
Lower Bristol Road
Bath BA2 3BH
England
Tel. +44(0) 800 136919
email: info@audiogo.co.uk
www.audiogo.co.uk

All our Large Print titles are designed for easy reading, and all our books are made to last.